The Legendary Auchinlea park

Gladigator
& the Legend of
Auchinlea

About the Author

Alex Richardson was born and raised in the tough housing estate of Easterhouse in the east end of Glasgow in 1960 . His early years like most youngsters of the area was embroiled in the gang culture and territorial disputes of the estate. He escaped the culture through the sport of weightlifting winning Scottish and British titles and founding the local weightlifting club from a coal cellar. From those humble beginnings in 1986 he has evolved the local club in to the modern day Gladiator childrens charity. The charity has won many awards such as the Queens award and the Glasgow buisness awards. Alex is now very much a major Ambassador for the local area and Glasgow. The charity is not dependant on donations and is fully self funded through delivering activites in play and sport. Gladigator is the charities mascot that engages with the children across all the charities services. The Gladiator charity delivers to locations throughout Glasgow and the Clyde valley and had over 250,000 attendances last year and growing. It has been a long term ambition of the charity to build its own indoor play area to generate regular long term income allowing the charity to sustaine its many free childrens services. It is hoped that the proceeds of the book can help raise much needed funds for the play area as well as increase awarness of the charities work, Alex commented. I had tremendous enjoyment researching all the local areas history and when you have run a childrens charity as long as i have i had no shortage of ideas for combining the fiction with history. We had a lot of fun filming the video for the book and writing the song to go with it. However having created Gladigator many years ago i am really excited that the book introduces his family for the first time that being Gladesgator and Agi & Tator the Agitators.

ALEX RICHARDSON

authorHOUSE®

Many people, including Glaswegians themselves, are only vaguely aware of the stories and legends associated with their great city. This is just one of those stories.

Quotation from the Glasgow coat of arms

There's the tree that never grew.
There's the bird that never flew.
There's the fish that never swam.
There's the bell that never rang.

Unquote

Welcome to the city of dreams and legends.
Welcome to Glasgow the dear green place.

Dedicated to my three gorgeous children
Lorraine, Daniel and Alex
And children everywhere

AuthorHouse™ UK Ltd.
500 Avebury Boulevard
Central Milton Keynes, MK9 2BE
www.authorhouse.co.uk
Phone: 08001974150

First published by AuthorHouse 6/23/2010

ISBN: 978-1-4520-3324-2 (sc)

This book is printed on acid-free paper.

The Bishoploch

CHAPTER 1

The Bishoploch

The place is the bishop's palace on the banks of the Bishoploch. The time is AD 1470. The loch is fed by the Molindiner burn, with its banks rumoured to have been widened to accommodate the Bishop of Glasgow's Venetian gondola, linking his palace in the centre of Glasgow to his country residence. The massive reeds that surround the loch stand out piercingly against the background of the white mist hovering over the loch, illuminated by the light of a full moon. Large shadows can be seen moving around the shores of the loch, projected by the camp fires surrounding it, which are manned by the bishop's guards, as are the five-feet-thick walls of the palace surrounded by a five-metre-wide mote. History tells the story of the marauders during the Reformation, and how the archbishop fled abroad to escape, whilst a local land owner demolished the palace brick by brick. However, there is history and then there is legend.

The bishop's guards have been over run in the silence of night, and they, along with the servants, have all been imprisoned in the palace's chapel, awaiting their fate. However, these marauders are of a nature which no one could ever comprehend. They are the original, mythical gladiators. Others would take their names and fighting styles through the centuries, but they originated in the hell of the Coliseum of Rome. Legends such as Myrmillo and Thracian, Essedarius and Andabatus, accompanied by their companions, evil Retarius, Dimachasurrus, Samnite, Laquerius, Secutor, and Velitus.

Together with their master they signed a pact with the devil to promote evil in the world. In return they would live for two millennia, during which they would have the opportunity to compete in history's battles and earn their rightful places as the protectors of Satan. They fought in the legendary war enactments of the Coliseum, where up to ten thousand souls perished in a day, all for the pleasure of Rome's citizens.

The Coliseum was not only the entertainment, but also the justice system. It kept public order. It also showed greatness for the empire, with emperors bringing strange exotic animals from the jungles of Africa, and fights between captured warriors from conquered armies.

Through the years the lust for blood became insurmountable, and the justice system needed little reason to sentence someone to the Coliseum to fuel the thrill of Rome. To these gladiators and their master, there was no good and no evil, only the thrill of battle. However, there was one foe that changed their fate, one foe that defeated them all in the Circus Maximus, in front of all of Rome. The emperor, in order to save face with the people, sent the gladiators to the mines of Africa as punishment. The mines quickly became their tomb when they were sealed in by an earthquake, robbing them of their right to fight in history's wars. It had taken them over 1300 years to dig their way out to freedom. Tonight they have tracked their rival down, and they will have their long-awaited revenge. However, their master also wishes to gain the gift bestowed on his foe by the Druids gods, a gift that is his and his alone to pass on – the right to have your age frozen in time. That foe is none other than the legendary children's champion, Gladigator. Their master is none other than the dreaded Tyrannous.

Tyrannous stands in front of the flaming and recently collapsed gate of the palace's perimeter, accompanied by Secutor and Retarius. 'The area is secure master,' says Velitus.

The silence of the night is disrupted by the angry scream of Tyrannous as he turns and shouts out to the palace, 'Surrender yourself and pass on the gift and you shall live. Come to me now and show yourself Gladigator. Don't make me come in and get you. I have your guards and their fate is in your hands.'

Tyrannous' shouts are met by a cold silence. 'Very well, Gladigator, the choice is yours,' he shouts. He turns to Velitus and says, 'Bring him to me.'

Velitus throws his flaming spear through the wooden flaps of a window, setting the room ablaze. Laquerius pulls on his battle rope and the sound of the palace door crashing to the ground is heard, accompanied by the screams of Secutor and Retarius entering the building.

Meanwhile, on the perimeter of the loch, the other gladiators stand guard. A sound of crackling in the woods is heard by Thracian. 'Is that you, Essedarius?' he whispers. As he turns his back to the loch, two small sets of hands suddenly appear through the mist, grabbing his ankles and pulling him in to the loch so quickly there was hardly a ripple on the calm surface. Essedarius heard the call from Thracian and starts to search in the direction of his voice.

He ventures into the reeds and looks down into the water, glaring at something that appears to be just under the surface. Suddenly a mighty hand grabs him by the throat and pulls him head first to the bottom of the loch.

On the other side of the loch, four other gladiators can hear the sound of a woman's voice coming from the woods, shouting for help. They enter the woods cautiously in the darkness. 'Over here,' calls the voice. Suddenly the night is awakened by large whipping sounds, and all four gladiators are left dangling in the air, hanging upside down from the trees, snared on the end of ropes. Their shouts can be heard through the night air back at the palace. Tyrannous turns to Laquerius and Valitus and snarls out an order. 'Go see to that!' Just at that moment, Secutor and Retarius can be seen in the distance coming out of the building, dragging a figure dressed in a white robe between them. They throw him to the ground and he kneels before Tyrannous.

'Where is Gladigator?' he asks.

'I don't know who this person is,' comes the reply.

'What is your name?' asks Tyrannous.

'I am Beaton, the Bishop of Glasgow.'

'Where is Gladigator?' Tyrannous asks, pointing his sword down toward the frightened figure.

Just then, in the middle of Tyrannous' angry shouts, a noise alerts Secutor and Retarius, and they turn round, noticing that Laquerius and Valitus have disappeared.

'I could have sworn I could see them in the distance. How can they be gone?' says Secutor.

Tyrannous turns round with a menacing smile and gives a mighty roar, Gladigator, show yourself; I have your bishop!'

Suddenly and silently, in the gap between the surface of the loch and the mist hovering above it, a figure begins to emerge. At first all that can be seen is a helmet. Soon massive shoulders, accompanied by a massive chest plate gleaming in the moonlight, appear, the water slowly dripping from it. The figure begins to talk as he emerges from the water.

'I have been expecting you! You took your time, though,' says Gladigator.

'Time is something we all have,' replies Tyrannous, 'but it is how we endure it that matters.'

'What is it? Who is it?' says the confused and frightened bishop, as Tyrannous throws him to the side.

'You two get rid of this one and the prisoners; they are no longer needed. I will see to our old friend. Are you ready to pass on your gift?' Tyrannous says, as he rushes toward Gladigator.

'Absolutely!' comes the reply, as Gladigator sends his battle hammer spinning through the black of night, hitting Tyrannous full on the helmet and sending him crashing to the ground.

Meanwhile, the two remaining gladiators head for the chapel, dragging the bishop between them. Suddenly from the bushes come the Agitators, swiping their legs from under them at great speed. A couple of simultaneous thumps to the head are delivered by Gladesgator, knocking them both out clean, accompanied by a shrieking voice shouting, 'Where do you two think you are going?'

The Agitators unlock the chapel and dash for the bushes as the bishop's guards run toward the palace, the bishop shouting, 'Find them and arrest them!'

By this time Tyrannous is back on his feet and invites Gladigator to follow him into the burning palace, 'You are comfortable in water, Gator. Do you dare to challenge me in the flames of hell?'

Gladigator nods and gives pursuit, slowly entering the building, surrounded by fire, and watching every corner in search of Tyrannous. Suddenly Gladigator is struck from behind by the flat edge of Tyrannous' battle axe, driving him face down to the floor.

'I could have pierced your armour,' shouts Tyrannous. 'Now pass on the gift; you do not have to die!'

At almost the same moment, Gladigator whips his powerful tail into Tyrannous' neck, sending him hurling through a collapsing wall.

Tyrannous comes springing out of the rubble and through the flames, placing both hands around Gladigator's neck. Gladigator does likewise.

'Pass on your gift?'

'Never.' says Gladigator, as he pushes his opponent through another wall.

'You must!' says Tyrannous, as he pushes Gladigator through the adjoining wall, surfacing in the main hall. The great and fine tapestries fall down, covering and blinding Gladigator. A massive crash of cracking timber and rubble, making a sound as if from hell, is heard as the roof comes down, taking the massive wooden stairway with it, and burying Gladigator beneath tons of rubble.

Tyrannous screams, 'Curse you, Gladigator! It looks like the gift will not be mine; however, the victory is.'

Tyrannous runs out of the blazing building into the cold, moon-lit night. 'The victory is mine,' he screams to his followers, 'Gladigator is no more.' He runs into the loch to cool his burning clothes and red-hot armour. He turns to face the bishop and his guards with his hands in the air. 'The victory is mine, you mortals!'

Just then the Agitators, Agi and Tator, and Gladys emerge from the bushes. 'What have you done with our father?' they cry.

'He is no more,' smiles Tyrannous, almost delirious with victory.

'Pops, where are you?' shouts Agi, 'Pops? Pops?'

Suddenly they are cut short by a horrendous scream from Tyrannous. At the end of his long ponytail is a hand from the lake, concealed within a scorched glove. 'Welcome to my world now,' says Gladigator. 'I have spent centuries preparing you a place.' And Tyrannous slips beneath the water.

A short time later, Gladigator reappears to the cheers of Gladys and the Agitators. The bishop and his guards are seen fighting the flames of the palace in a futile attempt to save it. He gathers up the rest of the gladiators one by one and pulls them to the bottom of the loch.

'I don't understand, Pops, says Agi. 'What have you done with them? They cannot drown because of their pact with the devil. Won't they come back?

'That's why we have to put them somewhere safe, where they can do no harm, until their pact ends in 2009 and they are gone forever.'

'That's why Tyrannous wants your gift, to have his age frozen in time?' asks Tator.

'Yes, so that he and his gladiators will not have to return to hell one day.'

'What have you done to trap them in the loch?' asks Agi.

Gladigator explains that the loch was once inhabited by a tribe in the Bronze Age, about 700 BC. They built a floating village, popular during that time, and lived in *crannogs*, or round houses. The people knew that wolves and other wild animals were scared of fire and water, and by building their huts on top of stilts above the water and linking them with walkways, they were safe from the animals, who could not swim, and would not be attacked or eaten in their beds.

'But what was to stop the animals from coming down the walkways?' Asks Tator.

'Fire!' says Gladigator. 'Big fires at the beginning of every walkway and the villagers also took turns patrolling the loch.'

Gladigator explains that the stilts that the village sat on top of were made of mighty oaks. Even if rival tribes were to burn the village during times of war, they could always build another one on top of the stilts. However, after hundreds of years, the stilts started to sink deeper and deeper into the loch, and eventually the village sank below the water. The timbers were gradually consumed by the sediment as well.

Gladigator went on to explain how the loch was situated over a bed of clay, as were miles of surrounding land. There are ancient lakes below the strong clay beds and one of the stilts had pierced a large hole through the clay. This may have led to the loch filling up rapidly, contributing to the ancient village being submerged. Gladigator tells how he dragged Tyrannous and his men under the clay bed and placed a massive boulder over the hole.

'Won't they be able to push it away, Pops?' asks Agi.

'No, son. The suction holding it in place makes it impossible to move. It could take them centuries to find another opening. We must never tell anyone of what has happened here. And we can no longer stay here; people will come to look for us.'

'Where will we go, Pops?'

We will swim down the Molindiner. There is a spot at Auchinlea where we can be safe, where there is high ground that we can build tunnels under.'

As they head off into the night, the bishop orders his guards and servants to not talk of what had happened. The church would not believe them and people could get in trouble. Some say the story of fleeing the Reformation was a front, as the bishop was known to rule Glasgow with an iron fist. Many believe that the events of that night frightened his very faith. Whatever his reason for leaving, the legend of the green lizard people was born and would be passed on for centuries to come.

CHAPTER TWO

Contact
The present day

'The house dates to 1492, and the defensive wall at the front of the house was built by the Hamiltons to guard against the Cromwell sympathisers. Mary, Queen of Scots, also stayed in the house,' said the tour guide, struggling to hear herself through the din of a restless party of local school children.

They are standing in the cobbled courtyard of the once splendid Provan Hall, a pre-Reformation house and the ancient county seat of the Glasgow lairds of Provan. Built as the residence of the Canon of Provan and Barlarnark, and later occupied by other nobility through the centuries, it sat in the middle of the spectacular Auchinlea Park, surrounded by paradise settings and unspoiled natural features dating back to the ice age. This paradise was bordered by the recently built Glasgow Fort shopping park that attracted 400,000 visitors per week, and surrounded for miles by the famous Easterhouse Estate built in the mid-1950s.

This was no ordinary day and the children were there for a very special reason – the new heritage centre built next to the old house was to be officially opened later that afternoon.

'Pay attention, children,' said the teacher, rather frustrated, as she had to turn her attention away from what was, for her, a rather exciting piece of history. However, whether it was exciting enough to hold the undivided attention of a class of eight and nine year olds was debatable.

'Leave me.'

'I never touched you.'

'Yes, you did,' came the reply, during one of their daily scuffles.

The laughter of the class was silenced by the teacher's loud intervention. 'Welcome to the world of Daniel and Alex, or as they are more commonly and affectionately known by friends and family alike, Dan the man, and Blondie.'

Suddenly, just as the teacher was coming up for air for another rant, her eye is caught by a rather pot-bellied figure grabbing the pair of trouble-makers by the arms and lifting them off the ground.

It was Steve Allan, the caretaker of the old house. He had been there for years and was an extraordinary historian when it came to the old house, with a passion to go with it. There was nothing that Steve did not know about the old place. However, despite this, he realised years ago that the grand tour was pretty boring to young kids, who would not understand the significance of local history until they were much older. But there was one story he would enjoy telling that was guaranteed to keep the children enthralled and have them looking twice at every nook and cranny.

'Has anyone ever heard the story of the green lizard people?' he interrupted.

All at once every little eye was focussed on him. He told the story of how mysterious lizard-type people had been sighted over the years, even during historical moments in time. Everyone assumed that Steve was pretending to the children, however he was always adamant that the story was true. Even more intriguing was the fact that only children had ever reported seeing them down through the ages. They all, later in their adult years, would try to prove to others their existence, but could never catch any other sightings. The story was passed down as a myth through the years, believed to be a creation of highly excitable children and continued through the years by other children claiming sightings through wishful imaginations.

'You never know, they may appear today,' said Steve, 'since this is another historic day for Provan Hall.'

Gasps of anticipation filled the air as the tour guide informed the children they were breaking for lunch in the gardens before the grand opening.

As the children enjoyed their lunch in the garden, the two intrepid adventurers, Dan the man and Blondie, decided to slip away, following the many trails into the forest that surrounded the old house. Dan, who was never happier than when he was noising up his younger brother, was continually running up ahead and hiding in the undergrowth, jumping out to surprise him. Blondie, as usual, eventually lost his temper and started to shout obscenities in his best, squeaky voice. On and on, in and out, Dan continued running, with Blondie following his trail of laughter in an attempt to find him. Eventually Blondie throws a stone into the undergrowth and hears a loud 'Ouch!'.

'You can see me? You can see me?'

'Yes, I can see you,' Blondie replied, as he ran full steam into the undergrowth.

What happened next seemed to last forever, but in reality lasted only a few seconds. He is stopped in his tracks by a green figure with big, beady, bright eyes, a small, long nose, slim shoulders supporting what appeared to be a small armoured vest and short battle dress, and a stump of a tail protruding above short legs and wide feet.

'It's one of the lizard people!' the green figure says, as he starts to run. 'It's the lizard people, Agi! Where are you? Agi?'

Blondie, still in a similar state of bewilderment, starts to shout the same words. 'It's the lizard people, Dan! It's the lizard people, Dan!'

Suddenly Blondie finds his jumper being pulled over his head and his legs being swept out from under him at great speed as Agi slide tackles him to the ground He can see nothing, but is aware of the sound of an accompanying voice shouting, 'Agi the conqueror strikes again.'

No sooner had Agi uttered those words when both he and Tator were sent crashing to the ground, in turn being greeted by the rather loud statement, 'And it's a sider from Dan the man, over and out.' Dan had been hiding from Blondie up a tree and grabbed the nearest long branch and swung down, hitting the Agi and Tator side on.

Dan the man comes to the rescue of Blondie as he
swoops down on Agi

The two figures are sitting on the ground and Dan is standing over them. Meanwhile, Blondie still has his head in his jumper, rolling around oblivious to what is going on, and screaming what he was going to do to Dan. He knew he had heard a strange voice, but with his mind not really believing what was going on, he chose to believe that his brother had decked him. Dan just stood in amazement, looking down at the two figures. Blondie popped his head out of his jumper and shouts, 'Now there are two lizard people!' Both he and Dan turned to run and heard a voice saying, 'Lizard people? We are not lizard people, we are the Agitators.'

Both lads turned around to find the figures were gone, only to be quickly tapped on the shoulders. 'How did you do that?' asked Blondie.

'Do what?' came the reply.

'You were behind us.'

'That's why we tapped you on the shoulder, stupid.'

No, I mean you *were* behind us.'

'Yes, and now we are in front of you.'

'Did you learn that trick watching wrestling?' asked Dan.

'What's that?' came the reply.

'Who are you? What are you?' asked Blondie.

'I am Agi, and this is my brother, Tator, and together we are the Agitators. Who are you?'

'I am Blondie, and this is my brother, Dan, and together we are the Ricky-canos.'

'Shut it, Blondie,' said Dan, quick as a flash.

'Why were you running?' Dan asked Tator.

'I was scared. I thought we were being chased by lizard people. Let's face it, the little guy has a gob on him.'

'I have got a gob on me?' said Blondie in his loud, squeaky voice.

'Try looking in the mirror, pal.'

'Why? What will I see?'

'A lizard! We just told you we are Agitators. Our dad is the mighty Gladigator from Rome.'

'This can't be,' said Dan. 'Gladigator is the mascot my dad dreamt up and created for his children's charity. Next you will be telling us your mother is Gladesgator.'

'She is. How did you know?' said Tator. 'What's your mother's name?'

'She's called Lizzy doll,' said Blondie.

'So you *are* descended from lizards!'

'Well, she does have some tongue in her head,' said Dan.

'Then maybe the little guy should look in the mirror.'

'So what will I see then?' asked Blondie.

'A goby wee boy!' said Tator.

Blondie goes into a silent, arms folded mood.

Dan interrupts, 'I still don't understand! My dad's charity has six Gladigator mascots and entertains thousands of kids up and down the country with them, in nurseries and schools and gala days.'

'Yes, and our dad walks amongst the crowd at the Auchinlea gala days and no one notices that there are seven Gladigators.'

'Is that so?' said Blondie. 'We thought by the smell that one of the mascot suits needed cleaned.'

Dan burst out laughing and placed a hand over Blondie's mouth. 'How can your dad be real if my dad invented him?' he asked.

'He did not invent him,' said Tator. 'I now realise who your dad is – he is Alex Richardson, the British Weightlifting Champion.'

'That's right,' said Dan, 'our dad is a legend, as well you know.'

'If you say so,' said Tator. 'However, both our dads have met, but yours was too young to remember.'

'This must have been a long time ago, because my dad is very old.'

'How old?' asked Tator.

'He is forty-nine,' said Blondie. 'What age is your dad?'

'He is 1900 years old,' said Tator. 'The only difference is your dad looks it.'

'What age are you two, then?' asked Dan.

'We are slightly younger, but our ages are frozen in time as a reward to our dad from the gods.'

'A reward for what?' asked Dan.

'For pledging to always look after and champion the children of the world. You see, the children of Rome persuaded the emperor to allow our father to live and gain his freedom for himself and his friends after he defeated the gladiators in the Circus Maximus.'

'"The Gladiators" is the name of our father's charity,' said Dan.

'We know, and it's all connected to when our fathers met,' said Agi.

'Why? What happened?'

'Your father was playing in the old White Rock quarry, which has been filled in now, where the shopping park now stands. He and his brother's friends made a raft out of an old gable door from the housing estate and paddled out in the quarry when he was four years old. Our father saved him when he fell in the water. Our father passed some of the magic on and that's why your father also looks after and fights for kids.'

'Does that mean our dad will live forever?' asked Blondie.

'Don't be stupid,' replied Tator. 'Your dad has grown old since then. However, you, on the other hand, will probably remain a little goby guy with a squeaky voice.'

'How did your dad manage to get from Rome to Scotland, and Auchinlea?' asked Dan.

'He would ride on chariots or horses he won in battle along the way, and sometimes he walked,' said Agi.

'I still don't understand. Why come to Scotland?'

'Unknown to the children of Rome, the emperor lied to them. He ordered his soldiers to give Gladigator a one-week start and then hunt him down,' explained Agi. 'The emperor was furious that Gladigator had defeated his gladiators, but did not want to show the children that it bothered him. Gladigator knew he had to get out of the Roman Empire in order to escape. He heard that the Caledonians were giving the emperor's army so much trouble that the emperor was considering building a giant wall to keep them out.'

'Is that Hadrian's Wall?' asked Dan.

'Yes,' replied Agi. 'Gladigator decided that if he gave the Caledonians a hand, then the emperor would have to build the wall and he would be free.'

'How did he fight all the other armies along the way on his own?' asked Blondie.

'He was not on his own; he won the freedom for all the creatures sent to the Circus Maximus that day and they followed him,' said Agi.

'How did they get their weapons?' asked Blondie.

'They stole them from the Romans. Some would save up swords, and others would save up shields,' said Agi.

'What did Gladigator like to save up?' asked Dan.

'Helmets,' said Agi. 'Our dad likes to look good, you know.'

'Ah ha! How did Gladigator get across the English Channel?' asked Blondie, with a cheeky grin.

'He put his friends in the boats and swam,' said Tator.

'What? He swam the channel?' said a confused Blondie.

'Well, he is a Gator, you clown' replied a smiling Tator.

'Who are you calling a clown?' said Blondie, with his eyebrows raised and joined together.

'Blondie, go and stand in a corner,' said a laughing Dan.

'Ah ha!,' said Blondie, forever trying to catch the Agitators out, 'How did you get by the ancient Brits?'

'Our mother, Gladesgator, used to be their Queen Bodicea.'

'Yes, and our mother, wee Lizzy doll, used to be the Duchess of Drumchapel,' Dan said, jokingly.

The Agitators looked on in confused silence.

'Ha, ha, ha, ha.' Blondie let out a huge laugh, having just caught on to the joke.

'Don't worry,' said Dan, 'he does that sometimes; it takes him a while.'

'Where was I?' said Tator. 'Oh yes, our mother was Queen Bodicea. She led the Brits into battle on her chariots.'

'But she poisoned herself rather than be taken alive,' Dan interrupted.

'No she didn't, that was someone else the Romans thought was her. She did not drink poison, she drank a potion prepared by the Druids before they cast a spell that changed her in to a Gator so that she would not be taken. However, she was captured by a travelling Roman circus and taken to Rome. It was before we were born. She escaped from the circus and met our dad in the forest in Italy.'

'Was it love at first sight?' asked Dan.

'No, more like love at first fight,' Tator replied. 'They were both trying to steal the same chariot. That's their passion, you see, they both love chariots. Anyway, how did your parents meet?' asked Agi.

'My dad had just returned from the world championships and wee Lizzy doll asked, "Ha, ha, big man, can I buy you a drink?" We get our drinks for free out of the Auchinlea pond,' said Tator.

'So you settled down in Auchinlea?' Dan asked.

'No, we arrived at the Bishoploch in the second century.'

'Ha, ha, ha, ha. Auchinlea pond?' said a hysterical Blondie.

'What did I tell you?' said Dan, as he put his hand across Blondie's mouth once again. 'My dad says he gets it from our Mum. Sorry.'

Agi gives them a cold, hard stare. 'Like I said before goby here interrupted, we settled down in Bishoploch. It had plenty of fish, and cold water to keep you cool in the summer. During the seventh century BC, the locals built a floating village and slept above the water; they would light fires at night around the loch to frighten the wolves away and to make sure they were not attacked in their beds. We stayed there until 1470. We were then discovered by—'

'Shuuuush! You know we are not allowed to talk about it,' said Tator.

'Yes, well we moved to Auchinlea during the fourteenth century and have lived here since,' said Agi. 'We were here when the Canon of Provan built the house. My dad was always on the lookout for Romans, as the Christians always attracted them.'

'Did you meet Mary, Queen of Scots, and her guards?' asked Blondie.

'Yes, we did.'

'What about the Hamiltons, who built the great wall to protect themselves from the Cromwell sympathisers?'

'They did not build the wall. That's what history claims, but my dad built the wall during the night to defend us against the Romans.'

'Where did he get the stones from?' asked Blondie.

'From the ruins of the bishop's palace,' said Tator. 'We lived under the raised mount behind the wall.'

'The bishop's palace? What was that?' asked Dan.

'You ask too many questions,' replied a frustrated Tator.

'I don't understand! The Roman Empire collapsed a thousand years earlier,' said Dan.

'That's why we had to move from the Bishoploch.'

Tator grabbed Agi by the throat. "Shuuush! I told you, Agi, we are not allowed to talk about it.'

'What about the children who have seen the green lizards over the years?' Dan enquired.

'They were the Baillie and the Hamilton families. We tried to play with them, but they always ran away. When they were older, they would pay people to hunt us down, but they could never see us.'

'Why was that?' asked Dan.

'My dad always said it was to do with their adult mind. Just like the adults in the Circus Maximus, their hearts were full of hate that prevented them from having a clear mind like the children have. That is why Gladigator is so pleased about the mascots your dad has in all the schools and nurseries,' enthused Agi. 'He says it is good that thousands of children see Gladigator so they won't be scared to play with us.'

'How do you know?' asked Dan.

'Well, you did not run away. The non-believing adults might one day believe as well,' he said. 'My dad says that the legend of Auchinlea is only a myth until the adults believe, and then it will be a real and magical place. One day the adults' minds will be clear like the children's, and there will be no more war, and there will be peace on earth.'

'But if your dad and you cannot die, why are you scared of the Romans or anyone else?' asked Dan.

'I did not say we could not die, I said our ages are frozen in time. We can still bleed, have an accident, and die. Or we can choose to pass the magic on.'

Just then the conversation was interrupted by the sound of the teacher calling for Dan and Blondie. 'There you both are! You could have got lost in here,' said the teacher, Miss Cameron. 'Who were you talking to, Blondie?'

Blondie turned round and pointed.

'A tree? So you were talking to a tree? Really?' said Miss Cameron.

Agi whispered in Dan's ear, 'What did I tell you about adults? They are as blind as a bat.'

Blondie asked, 'What is a bat?'

Tator said, 'That is what you will get in the mouth if you don't get back to the garden.'

The Agitators walked the boys back to the garden. 'We will stay on the edge of the forest and watch the ceremony. Come and see us again,' said Agi.

At that moment they introduced the speakers, Councillor Jim Coleman and Baillie McMaster.

'Oh no, it can't be!' says Agi.

'Yes, it is,' says Tator.

Both fall on the ground in hysterics. 'It is you know who,' says Agi.

'Who is it?' asks Blondie.

'It's the emperor and Mary, Queen of Scots.'

The Gladiator Programme main base

CHAPTER THREE

The Gladiator Programme

'Welcome, everybody, to the Hilton Hotel, for the most eagerly awaited event in the business calendar, the Glasgow Business Awards 2007,' said the announcer, news reader Jackie Bird. Glasgow was the economic hub of Scotland and this was the cream. The sound of continuous hand claps echoed across the magnificent ballroom. Over 300 of Glasgow's top entrepreneurs are decked out in their finest, and there is not an empty seat to be found around the elegant tables in the hall, despite the cost of £100 per time just to occupy a chair.

One table at the back of the hall boasts in attendance deputy leader Jim Coleman and Baillie Cathy McMaster, along with the chief executive of the Glasgow East Regeneration Agency, Ronnie Saez, and Mr Alex Weir from their economy team. However, amongst the noise and glitter, one man sits quietly in anticipation. He is a man that does not take losing well, and the stakes don't come much bigger than winning in this environment. The stakes are high for the founding member of The Gladiator Programme children's charity, none other than Alex Richardson.

This guy eats and sleeps Easterhouse, the beloved, but notorious, housing estate he lived in all his life. It was easier to count what he had not done for the local community, rather than what he had done. Get in to an argument about Easterhouse with him, and he would destroy you with an educated verbal assault backed up with an unprecedented passion for the area. He had travelled an unbelievable journey and tonight was just another step on that roller coaster.

He had run with a gang since he was four years old. He was there during the Frankie Vaughan gang armistice of the sixties that brought the local community international but unintentional infamy when he was eight years old. He had won numerous Scottish and British Olympic weightlifting titles and was ranked sixth in the world twice. He had produced hundreds of champions from the local community all the way up to British, Commonwealth, European, and world levels; he had also been Scottish National Coach.

But the success did not end there, not at all. He built a children's charity aimed at feeding kids into sports through play programmes, shielding them from the many social problems that blighted their areas. He only employed local kids that came through the programme. The charity had won distinguished awards, such as the Queen's Award and the Glasgow Community Champion's Award. However, despite those successes and the charity rising from a coal bunker to turnover close on one million pounds per year, Alex knew they would always be branded 'the little unprofessional group.' The Gladiators may have been a charity, but they did not depend on handouts. They were also a business, and earned their own keep. The Glasgow Business Award would silence the doubters out there and allow the charity to move forward. This was the big boys' event.

Suddenly the moment is upon us. The nominations are read out. His heart is pounding beneath his seemingly calm exterior. 'And the winner of the Social Economic Award for 2007 is The Gladiator Programme Limited.'

The silence is broken by rapturous applause. There was not a person in the room who did not hold affection for the Gladiators. After all, they delivered play services fronted by their Gladigator mascot to children in two thousand locations across the entire Clyde valley. He took his time walking to the podium as only Alex would, with flash bulbs going off all around. But even then the moment was already history – he was now thinking about where the charity was going next and their long-term goal of building a fun factory in Auchinlea Park. He thanked the sponsors and pledged to continue the fight for social justice and reminded the audience that there can be no greater investment for a community's future than in their children.

He arrives home somewhat worse for wear, clutching the award. He is greeted by Dan the man, 'Not another award, Dad.'

'What are you doing up so late?' asked Alex.

'We were waiting for you, Dad' said Blondie.

'We have had an unbelievable day,' said Dan.

'I know the feeling,' Alex replied.

'They have been excited all night and can't get to sleep, as they are desperate to tell you of their big adventure today,' said Liz.

'Big adventure?'

'Yes, the opening of the heritage centre.'

'Oh, right.'

'However, you won't believe what they have to tell you,' said Liz.

Alex follows the boy through to the bedroom and sits on the edge of the bed. He lies back pretending to listen to the boys' story and closes his tired eyes.

'We met Agi and Tator today,' said Blondie.

'Sorry, guys, we don't have the mascots yet, but I promise you we will have them next year.'

'No, really, dad, we met them. Gladigator is real,' Dan responded with excitement.

'Of course he is, Dan,' said Alex. 'He is real to all the boys and girls if they want him to be.'

'But he is real,' Blondie insisted.

'He came from Rome and fought in the Coliseum, and collected swords and shields and Roman helmets on his journey to Scotland,' said Dan.

Alex smiled, 'Well, of course he did, son.'

'He saved your life, Dad!'

Alex looked puzzled by the strange statement.

'He saved your life when you were four years old and fell in to the White Rock quarry,' Blondie continued.

Alex sat up on the bed; the boys definitely had his attention. He recalled being told of the incident at the quarry by his older brother who found him at the edge of the water. However, he could not remember himself. What really mystified him was how the boys knew, as he had never told them or Liz. It was something he had even forgotten himself until now.

'Gladigator passed his magic on to you, Dad, and that is why you fight for all the children,' said Dan.

'Can we leave it there for tonight, boys?' Alex insisted.

'It's getting late and we can speak about it tomorrow.'

Day breaks and it is Saturday morning. This is an exciting day for the community – it is the Auchinlea Gala day, and the Gladiators will be out in full force. The morning paper has just come through the door and Alex is settling down to read it at the breakfast table.

A small column catches his eye. Archaeologists discovered a cache of Roman weapons preserved in the mud and silts at the bottom of the Bishoploch during their search for a sunken village. The find boasts a collection of swords, shields, and an over-whelming variety of Roman helmets. The article went on to say that the search was for a medieval village, but the find would change how scholars viewed history, as the Romans were not thought to have settled so far north in Scotland. Alex remembers the boys mentioning Gladigator and his collection of weapons, and thinks to himself, How strange?

He checks the date on the paper; it is definitely today's issue. How could they have known, he wonders? Oh well, he smiles, and puts it down to coincidence.

One hour later and Alex and the boys are off to the Gladiator base. He takes the award from the night before to present to the workers at the team briefing for today's events. They enter the base through the shutters and Alex is greeted by Marc Ferns, the guy responsible for programming thousands of Gladiators events each year. 'We did it, Marc!' shouts Alex.

'You beauty!' comes the response, accompanied by a warm handshake.

Blondie and Dan enter the boardroom, and the entire Gladiator crew is there. 'Look sharp, it's the boss's kids,' shouts Dan.

'It's the terrible twosome,' came the response from a voice within the laughter.

Alex and Marc follow just behind. 'We did it, lads. We won the Glasgow Business Award,' shouts Alex, to a round of loud cheers.

All around the room there is silence as Alex describes the prior night's proceedings. These are the characters that make the Gladiators tick. There is Jack Rayton, the community manager, and Big Andy Gilbert, the marketing manager. Across from them are the two Tam Pincocks, father and son, they are the transport guys, the fixers, the jacks of all trades. Also present are the drivers, Jack and Billy, queuing up for their diesel costs from Carol Palmer, the administrator. Then there are the guys who are the Gladigator mascots, John Kelly, Jason and Rennie, Paul Cassidy, Sam Murray, and Clair and Paul Fitzsimons, and also all of the part-time staff, drawn from the local community, who will operate the theme toys.

The excitement over, it is time to go to work. All the vans are loaded, all the equipment checked, and it is time to ship out to Auchinlea. The sun is splitting the trees and the adrenalin is flowing with anticipation. Over ten thousand visitors are expected at the event. More importantly, the majority of them will be excited kids.

'Give them hell, lads,' shouts Harry Cooper, the chairperson of the Gladiator Programme, and one of the fittest seventy-four year olds out.

They get to the park and the lads begin preparing the activities. By 11 a.m., all safety checks and risk assessments are done, the vans are off-site, and they are preparing for the rampant hoards to come. There is the Triple Mega Challenge, all 232 feet of it, the Diddyman football, the Eliminator, the Duel, the double-lane Bungee run, and the Velcro Olympics. Also set up are the special needs section and a sensory challenge. There is something for everyone, including six Gladiator mascots working the crowds and dancing with everyone. By mid–afternoon, the park is busy with people and the pond is completely surrounded with the activities and children.

Alex is walking round the park with Dan and Blondie, jumping on every activity, and finally enjoying the day, since everything is going smoothly. He can see Dan sitting at the top of the chute on the Mega Challenge, looking around, as he has a view of the entire park. However, he is spending a lot of time up there and holding up the queue.

'Move your butt!' shouts Bible Billy, and Dan slides down the chute.

'He is here, Dad,' says Dan.

'Who is?'

'Gladigator is,' came the reply.

'I know he is, son. All six of him.'

'No, Dad, there are seven Gladigators'.

Alex looks around; it is hard to spot them all in the crowd. He is definitely counting six, all right, but Dan insists that one has just walked in to the forest area.

'It can't be, Dan, I count six. They are all present and correct.'

'I am telling you, Dad, one is in the forest.'

Alex agrees to enter the forest just to please Dan and prove that he is seeing things. By this time Blondie has appeared and is following close behind. The Agitators come out of hiding.

'We have brought our dad!' Blondie shouts.

The two boys disappear into the undergrowth and Alex continues down the narrowing and winding trail. 'Stay close to me now, boys, or you may get lost,' he shouts. Suddenly he can see the outline figure of a Gladiator walking toward him.

'Well, I'll be,' he thinks to himself,' 'I could have sworn all six Gladigators were out in the park. I wonder who it is.'

As the figure gets closer, Alex thinks, Wow, he is big. It must be Big Andy Gilbert in the mascot.

'You must be sweltering in that outfit,' says Alex, 'especially on a day like this, Andy.'

There is no response. The figure is standing toe-to-toe with him and must be seven feet tall.

'I hope you have the fan on to cool yourself,' says Alex.

The figure puts his hand on Alex's chest and throws him back about ten feet to the ground.

'What in the world!' says Alex, as he springs to his feet. This guy is strong! Alex knows strong; he competed in many weightlifting shows. 'Just who is in there?' he shouts, as he runs full force to the mascot.

The mascot dips to his knees to grab him, but Alex uses all the spring in his legs and stands on one of the mascot's knees, propelling himself up. He grabs the head, expecting it to come off and reveal the person inside, but it does not budge. Again he takes a run at the mascot. He stops short. The mascot swings and misses Alex and he jumps on its back, searching for the zipper at the back of the mascot, but it is not there. The mascot bends over and then stands up straight at great speed, sending Alex hurling through the air. Alex picks himself up. He has had enough of this, and his temper has gone.

He starts his final run. Suddenly he is brought crashing to the ground by two smaller creatures grabbing his legs at lightning speed. 'Agitators to the rescue!' they shout.

Agi looks up and says, 'Don't worry, Pop, we will save you!'

Suddenly Dan and Blondie come swinging out of the trees. Quick as a flash both Agitators hit the deck with a crashing thud. 'The two Ricky-canos strike again, over and out,' declares Dan.

Agi shakes his head. 'Not again,' he says.

The boys and the Agitators all get to their feet and start hugging each other. Gladiator lets out a roar-like laugh and Alex just stands there, open-mouthed and stunned.

'This just can't be,' he says. 'This just can't be.' He moves over and sits on a giant boulder protruding from the undergrowth.

'Do you believe me now, Dad?' Dan shouts excitedly. 'Do you see? Do you see? Do you believe me?'

Gladigator walks over and shakes Alex's hand and sits down beside him.

If I had known you were real, I would never have taken you on. I would have ran in the opposite direction,' said Alex.

Gladigator reaches into his battle dress and pulls out a small package , and stretches his hand out to Alex. 'Would you like a piece of gum?' he asks in a loud voice.

Alex just shakes his head.

Blondie says, 'I will eat it.'

'Shut it, squeaky, my dad's trying to be nice,' says Tator.

Gladigator grunts and Tator dives into the undergrowth.

'The boys say we have met before. They say you saved my life. Is that true?' asked Alex.

Gladigator nods his head.

'But my brother found me at the side of the water.'

'Yes, he did, but I placed you there for him to find you,' said Gladigator.

'How can my dad see you, Gladigator? He is an adult.' asked Dan.

'He has seen me before and I had to give him some of my magic to save him. His soul always could see me. I was always in his head. That's why he was able to create the mascots in my image. That's why he called the charity Gladiators. All adults can see me if they believe enough,' said Gladigator. "Every time I go to a gala day they all stop and shake my hand because they believe I am one of the mascots. They may not believe the Gladigator is real, but they believe the Gladigator mascot exists. The fact that their children love the Gladigator reminds them of their childhood and clears their minds. I used to be able to go to the Glasgow Fort shopping park for my shopping and no one noticed other than the kids. Their mothers would pull them away because they appeared to be talking to themselves. Now, because of the mascots making the adults believe, I am stopped for photographs every two minutes. One day the guy from one of the shops came up and offered me £20 if I would stand outside his shop for an hour to attract the kids. He said, "Don't worry I won't tell your boss, Alex does not need to know."'

'Is that right!' said Alex, and then paused. 'Sorry,' he says, shaking his head. 'Carry on. What were you saying?'

Gladigator explained to Alex how he had followed his career with interest and pride. He remembered when Alex was in the amnesty queue with Frankie Vaughan.

'You remember Frankie?' Alex asked.

The Gladigator started singing one of Frankie's hit songs. (*What do you want? If you don't want money.*)

The boys and the Agitators burst out in tears of laughter.

'Frankie was alright,' said Gladigator, 'He had the gift, a passion for kids, and he loved to entertain every one. You have the gift of the Gladigator qualities.'

'In what way?' Alex asked.

'I called my children the Agitators. The meaning of Agitator in the old Greek alphabet means many things, activist, campaigner, dissident, protester. Think of the many fights you have had with the politicians and sports authorities to stand up for kids and social justice. You always did it your way rather than conform.

You could never work for a public department,' said Gladigator. 'You like to change things. You like to win.'

At that moment they heard a screaming sound, getting louder and louder in the background. 'Right you lot, where are you?'

Gladigator jumped up, shaking. The Agitators were clearly agitated and shaking also. 'Coming dear!' Gladigator shouted. 'That's Gladesgator, my wife, shouting,' he whispered.

'We will meet again, won't we?' asked Alex.

Dan interrupts, 'Hang on a minute, that's our mum shouting, that's the Lizzy doll.'

Just at that she appears. 'Right you lazy lot!'

The Agitators dive into the brush, out of sight.

'If you think you are hiding in here while everybody else is working you have another think coming!' said Lizzy doll. 'As for you Andy Gilbert, get your butt out of that mascot and help the lads load the vans,' she ordered.

No sooner had she appeared and she was gone. 'I will give you five minutes!' she could be heard shouting in the background.

'PHEW! That was your mum?' Agi asked Blondie.

'Yes,' he replies. 'When she snores, the bed shakes.'

'That's just like our mum,' says Agi. 'When she snores, the ground shakes.'

'Do you know where the Gladiator sports base is on the other side of the park?' Alex asks Gladigator.

'Yes,' he replies.

'We will meet you there tomorrow.'

Suddenly the silence is shattered. 'Agi and Tator, get your butts back here now. Your dinner is ready. Tell that wimp of a dad when you see him as well!'

Gladigator starts to nervously retreat. 'This time it really is Gladesgator. I really have to go. I will see you tomorrow.'

Agi waves goodbye to Dan as Tator shouts to Blondie, 'I told you your mum sounded like ours.'

CHAPTER 4

The Recruitment

Sunrise on Sunday morning and Alex had arrived at the Gladiator sport base at Auchinlea. It must be the earliest he had ever risen on a Sunday. But the truth is he never slept a wink the entire night; he just could not get the previous day's events out of his mind. The Ricky-canos had heard him leaving and insisted on going with him. He left a note for Liz saying he was going into the office and the boys were going with him to play football on the Gladiator football park.

By the time they arrived, the boys were fast asleep. Rather than wake them, he left them in the car and entered the building. An hour must have come and gone, and Alex's eyes were starting to close, when he heard a bang at the fire exit door. He opened the door, and any last doubts that he had about the previous day's events were dispelled. There stood Gladigator, the rain running down his armoured vest.

'Could you not sleep?' Gladigator asked.

Alex shook his head.

'Neither could I.'

Gladigator entered the gym and crashed to the ground as he falls over a fully laden weightlifting bar.

'What a stupid place to leave a set of chariot wheels,' he raged.

Alex laughed. 'Yesterday I was in your environment, now you are in mine; you are the vulnerable one.'

They entered the office and Alex takes a seat. Gladigator separates the two adjoining desks to create a space for his tail and also takes a seat. 'Would you like a coffee?' asked Alex.

'Caffeine from the coffee bean? Not on your life, it hypes me up,' said Gladigator. 'No, it's all right, I have my gum.'

Both Alex and Gladigator remained silent and stared at each other for five minutes. Gladigator knew more answers than Alex, who was aware of this, but he thought it would be a moral victory if the Gladigator asked a question first. This was like a mental or ego-driven game of chess.

The silence is broken by Dan the man. 'Hi Gladigator.'

Gladigator nodded.

'Can I have the keys to the car, Dad? So that I can turn the heater on, it's cold out there.'

'Sure thing, son, but please let Blondie sleep.'

'OK Dad. Cheers.' And off he went.

Five more minutes went by and Gladigator suggested a game. 'I will say a word and you give a response with the first thing that comes to your mind. You say a word, and vice versa.'

Alex agreed, and Gladigator started the game. 'First word, battle.'

'Gang fighting!'

Alex said, 'Competition.'

'Coliseum.'

Gladigator said, 'Children.'

'Future.'

Alex said, 'Family.'

'Love.'

Five more minutes of silence went by.

Alex said, 'Tell me about competition. Tell me about the Coliseum!'

Gladigator sighed. Clearly something was weighing heavily on his mind, something uncomfortable.

'Sometimes it is good to talk,' said Alex.

'That is easy for you to say, you could talk for Scotland,' said Gladigator.

'Help me understand you.' said Alex. 'More importantly, help me understand what is going on with me. You saved me therefore you better start talking. You say you passed on your magic to save me, but I do not understand or ask for it. I need to know, and one day my family will need to know.'

At that point Gladigator began his story.

'I never knew my parents, or at least I don't remember them; I always felt alone. But for that reason I vowed my boys will never be alone. The Circus roamed the jungle of Africa capturing all the animals that the ordinary Roman had never seen. When I was a baby, I was part of the side show, as were all my friends. By the time I was fully grown, they were all dead. The ordinary Roman was no longer mystified by these indifferent creatures. They wanted more and more of a thrill; they wanted blood. I was carefully raised by my master. He protected me and taught me my skills and how to survive in the arena. Not because he cared, but for future profit.

'The Circus would travel from amphitheater to amphitheater. My matches were picked in the beginning, fights the master knew I would win. Then one day there was a new emperor appointed and he created the Gladiator Grand Prix. He figured it would win him over with the people and the winners and heroes could represent his army and bolster the conquests of his empire, particularly in the north of Britain, the dreaded Caledonians, known today as the Scots. The standard of competition jumped up, of course, and suddenly the empire went crazy.

'Anyone who was anyone was desperate to fight in the Coliseum, or race in the Circus Maximus. The competition attracted the best and the worst of everyone. I made the final at the Circus Maximus, but I paid the price. All of my team, with the exception of Harry, the horse who pulled my chariot, were gone. I would be fighting the emperors's finest, led by Tyrannous, who was said to be feared by the gods. He was not the emperors's equal, but the emperor preferred to appease him and paid him well – better to have him on your side than defer your attention from running an empire to fight him.

'Legend has it that Tyrannous made a pact with the devil; others believed he was the devil. The emperor new that Tyrannous loved the thrill of the Coliseum. He could kill anywhere, of course, but not in front of an audience of so many and so blood thirsty as this. Legend had it that he had a fatal weakness, but no one had ever got close enough to find it. He was ruthless. He believed that if you got rid of little children, then the rest of the population would grow old, and no one would grow up to fight him. I had never met him, but that taught me he was a cold-blooded coward!'

The Gladigator's story continues with his arrival in Rome.

Gladigator arrived in Rome with a little over a week to prepare and find his new team. He went to the local magistrate's court to await sentence for the poor individuals that fuelled the thirst of the Coliseum and the Circus Maximus on a weekly basis, arriving in court in time to hear the shout of a centurion announcing, 'Hail the emperor! Would all be upstanding for Senator Rayton?'

The senator spoke, ' 'OK. Send in the first case. Call Ram Ses? Call Ram Ses? Who is the duty representative of the defendants today?' asked the senator.

'I am, my lord,' said Politico Correctness.

'It had to be you!' said the senator. 'OK, tell me your story Mr Ses.'

'My lord, senator, I was, until a year ago, the emperor's accountant. I am a descendent of a long line of accountants, dating back thousands of years. We built the temples of the gods at Abu Simbel in ancient Egypt; we were responsible for counting the stones. The building work was started by the Great Pharaoh Ramses II and lasted almost fourteen hundred years, spanning the lifetime of more than thirty pharaohs. My family took the name of Ramses. That is why I am called Ram Ses. We were made redundant during the Roman occupation and sent to Rome to work on the city. We have worked under all the emperors for the last four hundred years.'

'Spare me the history lesson and get on with it, man,' said Senator Rayton.

"I object, your eminence!' said Politico. 'My client is not a man, he is a goat.'

'I stand corrected. Now get on with it!' said Senator Rayton.

'The emperor and I had a falling out and he sent me to count the bricks during the building of Hadrian's Wall.'

'That must have been some fall out,' said the senator.

'I was undermined by his current accountant, your eminence,' said Ram.

'Well, who might that be?' asked the senator.

"None other than Devine Intervention, my lord.'

'Well, he certainly intervened on you,' said the senator, 'but why are you here today?'

'I had been counting the bricks on sections of the wall at a rate of five thousand a day, of which I would mark and keep a stone in my basket to represent each day. We would not let anyone build beyond five thousand per day. But, Hadrian had heard that the emperor was ill, and since he was next in line to be emperor, he was keen to finish the wall, protect his future empire, and return to Rome.

'He started to speed up the building of the wall, leading to much unrest. The Roman council had insisted he employ their workers. Of course, that led to union problems on the account that no one knew who's job it was; for a variety of things, it was never anyone's job, but Hadrian believed it had to be somebody's job. "I will get my shop steward in, I work for the council, and it is not my job," they would say.'

Loud snores are heard. 'My lord, Rayton, please wake up,' said Politico Correctness.

'What? Okay then, get on with it man.'

'Err, goat, your eminence.'

'Yes, whatever.'

Ram continued, 'I was counting the bricks and trying to project how many we would need to finish the job and forward plan, and just how many labourers, plus time and effort multiplied by the cost and the amount of food to feed them, it would take to bring the project in under budget.'

'For god's sake, man, talk normal to me and get to the point,' interrupted the senator. 'What happened?'

Ram apologises and continues the story, 'Hadrian happened to be inspecting the wall with his council, when he speaks to a commander behind me, asking for a progress report.

"There are seven million, two hundred and twenty thousand bricks to go, your excellency," he is told.

Hadrian then pointed at me and asked, "How many bricks to go?" I replied, "I don't know! You interrupted me and I have lost count." "Lost count?" Hadrian screamed. I repeated that, "Yes, I lost count."

Hadrian turned to his guards and told them to send me to the Coliseum. I tried to tell him that I am the emperor's accountant, and that he had sent me here to count the bricks. But he told me to count myself lucky he was only sending me back to the Circus Maximus.'

Senator Rayton asked Ram, 'Are you finished?'

'Yes," he replied.

'Well, you obviously gave a good account of yourself, but at the end of the day, I do not have time for all this. You can always count on me to make the right ruling, therefore I sentence you to the Circus Maximus. Now take him away!'

Ram is dragged, screaming and shouting, 'I hope Senator Rayton realises I will hold him accountable for this!'

'I am sure you will. Next defendant.' Senator Rayton shouts. "Call Thomas Peacock Senior and Thomas Peacock Junior? Just talk to me and keep it short.'

Peacock Senior takes the stand. "Your honour, you are supposed to get from the first of the month to the end of the month to make good any faults on your chariot highlighted from your safety, test certificate. My wife counted that could be up to thirty-one days, which would mean she could afford to visit her sisters and her pay would be in the bank the following day. We were only gone twenty-nine days. We booked the chariot in for the 30th.'

Senator Rayton interrupts, 'This is February and there are only twenty-eight days; there is no 30th.'

'I told you it was February, Dad; I told you,' said Peacock Junior.

'Thomas, don't argue with me,' said Peacock Senior. 'But dad—'

'Enough of this,' said Senator Rayton. 'The last guy could count, you lot cannot count. I hope the next guy understands English. I am having a bad day. Now take them to the Circus Maximus.'

Senator Rayton called for the next defendant 'Call Bible Billy the kid? Call Billy the kid? Not another goat!' said Senator Rayton.

In walks Bible Billy the kid, a baby goat standing on two legs, wearing a holster on both hips and a cowboy hat.

'Name?' asks the clerk.

'Let me explain who I am and I will change your life.'

The clerk interrupts, 'Name?'

'Bible Billy the kid.'

Senator Rayton said, 'Now let's not muck about here, son, and spare me the history lesson. There is something wrong with you, you know that, now talk.'

'I am a gum slinger,' said Billy.

'How do you sling gum?' asked the senator.

'I follow a tradition dating back to David and Goliath, when he slew the giant with a stone on his sling,' answered Billy.

Senator Rayton cut him off. 'Now I am trying hard here, son, so explain to me, in not too much detail, why you are here.'

Billy repeats, 'I am a gum slinger.'

'What type of gum do you sling?' asked Senator Rayton.

'Gum from the gum tree, your eminence!'

'Can we cut to the chase?' said Senator Rayton. 'Why are you here?'

'This lot lifted me for dropping chewing gum on the street,' shouted Billy in an angry voice.

'But you have almost admitted the crime,' said Senator Rayton. 'Why should you not go to the Circus Maximus?'

'Because I did not drop it, I slung it,' said Billy.

'Can I ask you a question, although it has absolutely no relevance to the case?' asked Senator Rayton.

Billy nods.

'Why do they call you Bible Billy?'

Billy smiles and replies, 'That's obvious – because I swear on the Bible I did not commit this crime!'

'Take him away; I am going home,' said Senator Rayton. 'These Christians are driving me mental.'

Just then Politico Correctness suggested to Senator Rayton that he felt his clients did not have a fair hearing.

The senator responded, 'You failed to call any witnesses in any of these cases. This is Rome. Are your clients wealthy?'

'No, your eminence.'

'Then there are no witnesses.'

Politico responds in his best politically correct jargon trying to win over the senator's conscience in a vain attempt to get him to reconsider.

'It is for that very reason, my lord, that you should try to land that spear in that box; you should attempt to steer that chariot home. The falcon on the emperor's staff flies no more.'

Senator Rayton intervened, 'If you were a falcon with a staff stuck to the bottom of you, would you be able to fly? Try driving the chariot when the box is on the top of your head with a spear in it.'

Politico responds, 'I beg to differ, my lord.'

'You would, Politico, but you stand corrected. This court is closed.'

As Gladigator left the magistrate's court, Harry the horse said, "That's it then; we are done for. This time next week I will be dog food."

Gladigator thought that these guys had qualities; but was unsure how he could use them. They went to the cells in the Circus Maximus to view anyone they had missed the day before. It was there that they met the tallest person either had ever seen.

'What's your name?' Gladigator asked.

'I am Big Scot the giraffe.'

Howls of laughter echoed around the cell.

'Don't ask,' said Scot.

'I have to,' replied the Gladigator, with his armour jumping up and down nine to the dozen. 'Why not George?'

Scot cut in, 'Or Jerry? I have heard it all before.'

'Can you lift a horse or a chariot with a rope around your neck?' Gladigator asked.

Scot said, 'Of course.'

'You are on my team,' Gladiator declared. 'Ram you will be my time keeper on the laps of the chariot race. You two Peacocks will be my mechanics during the pit stops.'

'I could ride your chariot if you pay for the water for the horse,' Peacock Junior cried.

'Shut it, Thomas,' said his dad.

"But I will."

"Thomas, don't argue with me," said Peacock Senior.

Harry the horse flared up, "That's it, I am out of here! You are going to place your trust in this lot against Tyrannous?"

"Should we not get a message to mum?" asked Peacock Junior.

"If we win our freedom, you can go home if you like, but I am backing Gladigator," said Peacock Senior.

Just when things could not get any lower, the Gladigator went home that night to a major surprise – a shiny state-of-the-art chariot called the Rayton Rocket.

The deliveryman told Gladigator, 'The Senator is sympathetic to your plight, but he hopes he has sent you the right people for the job with his sentences.'

Harry the horse was over the moon. 'We now have a chance of winning,' he said. 'However, I have to tell you something I found out this morning: Steve the stallion will be driving for Tyrannous.'

'That's all right,' said Gladigator. 'He is one of the good guys.'

'You don't understand,' said Harry. 'The chariot he will be pulling is a Wheel McKay, made in Scotland.'

'You're joking!' said Gladigator.

'Worse than that, it was built on Clydeside.'

CHAPTER 5

The Circus Maximus

The team only had a few days to prepare for the tournament and rehearse the pit stops for the chariot race. The rules allow a one-minute pit stop during the race. During that time, the hose has to be connected to water the horse; a shoe or a broken rein may have to be replaced; the chariot may need a new wheel or a floor panel repaired; and Gladigator may be injured or require a change of weapons. Harry is inspecting the surface of the arena, searching for any hidden pop-ups or potholes that could crush a wheel or throw a horseshoe. Ram Ses is in charge of keeping the infantry of equipment and spare parts.

The Peacocks are discussing the chariot and connecting a new proto-type suspension made up of two large springs they had made by a blacksmith; no one knew if it would work, but Peacock Junior was thrown through the thatched roof of the blacksmith's shop while they were making them. Scot would be responsible for passing the weapons to Gladigator from the pits as the chariots raced by – timing was of the essence, although the big fellow had an ideal advantage as he could hang over the pit and had a superior reach.

The big day of the event arrived and all of Rome was buzzing with anticipation of the battle of two undefeated warriors: the children's champion Gladigator against the council of Rome's champion Tyrannous. The prizes are freedom for Gladigator and his team, and the reward of leading one of Cesar's armies for Tyrannous. The flags are hanging all round the top of the Circus Maximus, barely moving in the wind. The blazing sun illuminates the arena. Agi and Tator are in the stands, leading the singing children. Gladesgator sits in the segregated end, surrounded by fifty centurions wearing ear plugs.

Normally there would only be chariots drawn by either four horses or seven horses in the races. It was very unusual to have chariot races drawn by a single horse, but this was no ordinary race. These two warriors were undefeated in the Coliseum and amphitheatres all over the empire. The whole of Rome wanted to see this battle. The Coliseum only held fifty thousand people, but the Circus Maximus held well over one hundred and fifty thousand people.

Harry the horse is pacing up and down, waiting to be strapped in to the chariot, as is Steve the stallion.

'Let's make it a good one, Steve,' said Harry.

'I don't have to be here, Harry, this is not my job. I should be out in the street pulling taxis,' said Steve.

'That is what happens if you take a job with the council,' replied Harry.

Billy the kid asks some of the attendants if they can help with moving the equipment to the pit enclosure.

'Sorry, I can't help you mate, it's not my job. I just collect the tickets. You would have the union down on me,' came the reply.

'Who is in charge?' asked Billy.

'No one,' came the reply, 'this is the Circus Maximus.'

The emperor at last takes his seat, accompanied by his accountant Devine Intervention, who is frantically adding up the gate receipts.

'This is going to be big, your excellency. We have made a fortune. I suggest that if Gladigator loses, you let him live. A rematch would bring another great day! It will be an economic disaster if Gladigator were to win his freedom.'

'If he wins, he will be going nowhere,' said the emperor.

Down in the arena the Gladiators stand along the inside of the track. They will attempt to knock Gladigator off his chariot as he rides by.

Down below, in the entrance of the arena, Gladigator has mounted his chariot and is going through some last minute preparations with the Peacocks.

'Now, I have put a note next to these two buttons,' said Peacock Senior. 'It reads "only to be used in an emergency",'

'What do they do?' asked Gladigator.

Just at that point they are interrupted by Tyrannous mounting his chariot. 'You there, give me your sword,' he shouts to the centurion standing next to the chariot.

'I can't,' said the centurion. 'This sword is council property.'

Tyrannous cracks his whip and the chariot jumps forward. With the wheel parked on top of the centurion's foot, Tyrannous reaches over and grabs his sword. 'You won't be needing it now,' he roars.

Gladigator draws up beside him. 'That sounded like a sore whiplash there, Steve,' said Harry.

'It was, and we haven't even started yet,' Steve replied. 'Let's hope this is over quickly.'

Up top, the emperor gives the signal for the competition to begin. The doors to the arena open up to the frantic noise of the crowd, as the piercing light shoots in, breaking the darkness.

The two warriors are revealed in all their glory. The shining armoured chest plate of Gladigator, with his massive tail that could snap a man in two, his gleaming helmet, and, of course, that massive smile that all the children adored. Next to him is his opponent, the assuming Tyrannous, a man-mountain standing almost eight feet tall, with a long ponytail of hair dropping down from the back of his helmet. Half gorilla, half man, with protruding, jagged teeth, and glaring eyes, he has massive muscular arms, and his wristbands have small spikes on them. Below his chest armour is a small waist supported by massive thighs that are as thick as a man's waist.

Tyrannous notices Gladigator staring intently at him. 'Do you have anything to say before we do this?' he asked.

'I like your helmet.' said Gladigator.

Tyrannous draws him a cold stare and cracks his whip. His chariot enters the arena, closely followed by Gladigator. Both chariots take their positions on the start line, awaiting the playing of the national anthem of Rome. Up in the commentary box, the excitement is continuing to mount. The commentator makes his announcement, 'Welcome fight fans and chariot race lovers from across the empire. This is the main event of the evening. Ten rounds of the arena here in the plush Circus Maximus of Rome. Let's get ready to grumble! It's show time! Our opponents today need no introductions.'

Down on the track, the Gladigator team is going through the last minute preparations. 'Now listen,

Harry, stay on the inside going round the bend and come across to the outside on the straight ways. We need to keep as much distance as we can from the Gladiators in the middle of the arena,' said Gladigator.

'You will have to help me,' says Harry. 'When I shout left, you have to shift your weight to that side of the chariot; if I shout right, you do the opposite.'

'Remember now.' says Peacock Senior, 'keep your hands of those buttons unless you have to.'

'That's right! I was going to ask you—'

Boom! The start drum echoes out.

'They're off and running,' says the commentator, as Tyrannous almost knocks Gladigator clean out of his chariot.

As they barely start to move, Gladigator only just hangs on to the right side of the chariot. Harry has his head down, 'We are coming to the first bend. Move to the left. Are you deaf? I said move to the left!'

'Out comes the first of the Gladiators, Retarius, to throw a net over Gladigator,' said the commentator. 'Wow! The chariot goes in to a spin and knocks Retarius clean in to the stanchions. Gladigator regains control of the chariot.'

'Am I talking to myself?' shouts Harry.

'You were for a minute,' replies Gladigator, 'but we are all right now.' 'Get alongside Big Scot at the pit.'

'Drop me the ball and chain,' he shouts to Big Scot, who obliges.

The commentator continues, 'Tyrannous is closing on Gladigator from the inside. He is about to strike with his sword. The second Gladiator, Velitus, is about to strike from the opposite side. Gladigator only has two arms. He blocks Tyrannous with his shield and jams his sword into Tyrannous' wheel, taking out one of his spokes. At the same time, he catches the ball and chain with his tail and wraps it around Velitus' hammer, pulling him onto the track. The hammer and chain follow through, hitting Tyrannous full on the face!'

'Jump, Harry!' shouts Gladigator.

Harry jumps over Velitus and the chariot hits Velitus full force.

'Wow!' says the commentator, as Tyrannous' chariot wobbles back to the centre of the arena and he barely hangs on.

The children in the crowd are going crazy and chanting Gladigator's name, much to the disgust of the emperor.

'Remember, folks, Gladigator has to beat off the Gladiators and come over the line before Tyrannous to win the race,' says the commentator. 'We are coming up to the second lap, now.'

Down on the track, Gladigator asks, 'How was that, Harry?'

'I have had worse first laps, but you have to keep your mind on the job and stop waving to the children. This guy is dangerous!' said Harry. 'There is something going down.'

'What do you mean?' asked Gladigator.

'Steve is slowing down.'

The commentator breaks in, 'There are two Gladiators, Samunite and Myrmillo, holding up a rope of spikes!'

Meanwhile, back on the track, Harry warns, 'Watch yourself! I can't avoid them.'

Gladigator presses one of the buttons and the suspension springs him up into the air, and over the rope of spikes as his chariot passes under it. He falls back down lands on top of Tyrannous' chariot. Gladigator hangs on with one arm and takes a pounding from Tyrannous.

'Wow!' says the commentator.

Back down on the track, Gladigator screams for Harry to come alongside him.

'Let me through or I will knock you clean over,' Harry says to Steve the stallion. 'You don't need this hassle; you will get no thanks from the council.' Steve obliges and Harry pulls alongside and Gladigator jumps back onto his chariot. Meanwhile, they are coming round to the spiked rope again. Bible Billy the kid draws his two slings, hitting the two Gladiators with gum and blinding them, causing them to lower the rope. But they are stuck to the rope by the gum and can't let go.

As Gladigator's chariot runs over the rope, he bends down and catches the middle of it. He drags the two Gladiators into the centre of the track and lets them go. Tyrannous' chariot runs over the top of them and almost tilts over.

'Four Gladiators are gone and both chariots have taken a beating. Not surprisingly, both teams are coming in for a pit stop,' came the commentary.

'We are coming in! Get ready!' shouts Harry the horse. They enter the pit and everyone goes to work. Ram sticks the hose into Harry's mouth and he is sucking on it like a straw and talking at the same time.

'I have lost my front two shoes,' he shouts to Billy the kid.

'Don't worry, Harry, I have never lost a horseshoe throwing competition in my life.'

Harry lifts up his front two legs and Billy slings the shoes on. Meanwhile, the Peacocks have their own problems with the chariot. 'I told you to try and avoid pressing the button. Now I need to repair the floor,' shouts Peacock Senior.

Big Scot holds the block and tackle over the chariot and Peacock Senior hoists it up. 'You see to the undercarriage floor, and I will change the wheel,' he shouts to Peacock Junior.

Meanwhile, Gladigator is loading another sword and a hammer into the chariot. The Agitators arrive in the pit. 'Nice going, Pops!' said Agi. 'Can we have some money to go to the hamburger stall?'

'Not now.' smiles Gladigator. 'Can't you see I am in the middle of something.

Scot releases the chariot and it crashes down. Ram removes the hose. Gladigator shouts, 'Check?' The crew all respond, 'Check!' Gladigator cracks the whip and Harry the horse shoots out of the pits at lightning speed, roared on by the crowd.

Back in the commentator's booth, 'It's Gladigator who comes out first in a brilliant time of forty-four seconds. And Tyrannous follows close behind. There appears to be some friction with the Roman guards in the crowd, but it's okay now. It was only Gladesgator jumping up to clap her hands as Gladigator came out of the pits. These Roman guards are beginning to get a bit nervous as the crowd starts to believe that Gladigator might just win this. However, there is still a long way to go, so let's get back to the action! They are coming around the bend to begin the ninth lap. Oh! And what's this? Tyrannous' team has fitted their chariot with blockers on the wheels. They are moving in and out in a punching motion and will soon be punching away at Gladigator's wheels.'

Down on the track, Harry shouts, 'We're coming level with those blockers!'

'Find me a gap; you have got to find me a gap, Harry,' shouts Gladigator.

The two chariots are side by side. Harry moves to the left and his chariot wheel is brushing the wall. But the gap opens up. Gladigator drives his battle hammer down hard from above his head, knocking the blocker clean off Tyrannous' wheel. The two chariots come back together, and Gladigator drives the end of his hammer clean into Tyrannous' chest, almost knocking him to the ground, as Harry starts to pull away.

'This is it!' shouts Harry. 'We are coming up to the last lap; they are going to throw everything at us.'

The commentator continues, 'Well, this is it, race fans, the moment of truth as we enter this final lap. Who will still be undefeated in a few moments time? Here we go! As we come out of the first bend, it's Gladigator in the lead. Wait a minute! We have ten Gladiators forming a triangle with their shields up. They will try to force Gladigator to swerve and allow Tyrannous' chariot to catch up. But wait a minute! The Gladigator is kneeling on one knee. He has his hand hanging over the edge of the chariot, with what looks like a large steel ball. Oh my god, he rolls it! Is it going to be? It is! It's a perfect strike and the children in the crowd go berserk.

'Tyrannous' chariot is catching up. But wait a minute! There seem to be obstacles appearing in their path, forcing them to swerve all over the place. They are soldiers; they are definitely soldiers! Hold on, it's Gladesgator. She is throwing Roman guards down onto the track from the stand! It's all kicking off here now, race fans, as we pass the second bend.'

Back on the track, Gladiator says, 'You know what to do, Harry.'

'Yes, don't let the wheel with the blocker get on our inside.'

'Okay, take us home.'

Back to the commentator, 'Okay, folks, they are coming out of the third bend. There are two archers standing cocked and ready to fire! I don't think the Gladigator will see them until he passes the bend. Hold on a minute! Out come the Agitators to sweep the legs from under them!'

Back on the track, they are coming out of the bend. Harry shouts, as he comes out of the bend, 'It's the Agitators!'

'You can't hit them, Harry!' Gladigator shouts.

Harry slows down and swerves in and out to avoid the Agitators, almost sending Gladigator out of the chariot.

'Phew! That was a close one,' says Gladigator. 'Watch yourself, they're coming level, Harry. They are on our inside.'

'I know; I could not do anything about it,' shouts Harry.

Tyrannous pulls level and his blockers punch away at Gladigator's wheel. Gladigator plunges his long fork into the wheel of Tyrannous' chariot.

'This is it as we come out of the final bend!' says the excited commentator. 'Someone's wheel has got to give!'

Suddenly Tyrannous' wheel gives way and his chariot crashes upside down. Steve the stallion bolts away. But the Tyrannous has managed to jump onto Gladigator's chariot.

Gladigator is on his belly and Tyrannous is on top of his back with his hands around Gladigator's neck, pushing his face down onto the track. Gladigator wraps his whip around the side of the chariot and wraps the reins around his other hand. He presses the button on the dashboard of the chariot with his long tail. Both are propelled up into the air. Tyrannous flies fifty feet in the air and crashes to the ground as the chariot heads for the finish line. Gladigator is pulled back down by the whip and the reins and summersaults onto Harry's back. They cross the finish line with Gladigator holding his hands aloft.

The children in the crowd are ecstatic!

'It's over! It's over!' says a rather hoarse commentator. 'This race is over fight fans. Gladigator has tamed the Circus Maximus of Rome.'

Tyrannous lies face down on the track, surrounded by the emperor's guards, twenty spears pointing down at his back. Harry starts fox trotting as they take their lap of honour. Gladigator has his toothbrush out and is brushing his teeth and pretending to scratch his back with it. The kids start cheering as he spins it on his nose. The chariot draws to a halt below the emperor's throne.

The emperor waits for the crowd to go silent so that he can present the winner with the victory wreath. 'I can't let Gladigator go,' says the emperor in a rage.

Devine Intervention leans across and whispers in the emperor's ear, 'This might be none of my business, but your popularity could crash at the next election and your old friend, Hadrian, would take your throne. If you are liked by the kids, you are liked by the people.'

'What should I do?' asked the emperor.

'Send Tyrannous to hard labour in the African mines, then free Gladigator and hunt him down a week later. By the time everyone finds out he is gone, they will believe he was lost in battle fighting for the children of Rome!'

'That is a fantastic idea!' said the emperor.

'It is your idea,' said Devine.

'Yes, quite,' said the emperor. 'Can you do the honors?'

'Yes,' said Devine. He then rose to his feet and read out his scroll: 'Silence in the big Circus Maximus! I am Devine. The next person to win his freedom from the big Circus Maximus arena is Gladigator!'

The children's cheers drowned out the booing of the adults. As Gladigator leaves the arena, Bible Billy is thanking the Lord. The two Peacocks are asked by the attendant if they would like to stay behind to clean up the arena. Peacock Senior says, 'Not me, mate, I don't work for the council and I am a free man.'

Peacock Junior shouts, 'I will stay for an hour if you like,' much to the confusion of his dad, as he drags him away.

That is the story of how Gladigator and his family, backed up by the two Peacocks, two goats, a giraffe, and a horse became the heroes of every child in Rome. However, their adventures were only just beginning.

CHAPTER 6

The Holiday

'What an incredible story!' Alex says to Gladigator.

He had sat open-mouthed through the whole story. So much so that he forgot that he had left the kids in the car. However, unknown to him, the Agitators and the kids had taken the car for a drive round the Auchinlea pond while he was listening to Gladigator's story.

Back in the car, Blondie has woken up to the sounds of the Agitators quizzing Dan the man. 'How do you make this chariot go without a horse?' asked Agi.

'You have to turn the key,' said Blondie.

Tator turns the key and the engine comes on, along with the radio, startling both the Agitators, who jump into the back seat and land on top of Blondie.

'Stop it,' Blondie says.

'Sorry,' replied Agi.

'But how do you make this chariot move?' asks Tator.

'You have to press the pedal,' laughed Dan.

Tator bends down to press the pedal. The engine lets out a roar. Tator jumps up and sticks his head through the steering wheel and Agi once again lands in the back on top of Blondie.

'Okay, Tator, you stay down and hold the pedal and I will drive,' says Agi.

'You have to press the other pedal; that is the clutch to change gear,' said Dan. 'That is the gear stick beside you.'

'Okay, we have got the hang of it,' said Agi, as the car whizzes away at great speed toward the pond in Auchinlea Park. The radio is belting out the theme tune from the old Gladiator television show.

As the car sped round the pond, the Agitators are laughing and having a ball. Suddenly they swerve and drive in to the pound and land on the island.

'I don't think my dad is going to be too happy about this,' says Blondie.

The lads walked back to Auchinlea to inform their dad. But Alex is too engrossed in Gladigator's story to listen.

'Don't interrupt!' he shouts to the boys.

'But Dad, there is something you should know,' says Dan.

'Look here are the keys to the football park. Why don't you go for a kick about,'

'Okay then,' said Blondie, and off they went.

'I am sorry about that,' Alex said to Gladigator. 'Please continue your story.'

The day after the Circus Maximus, backed up by his prize money from winning, Gladigator decided to treat his family and friends to a holiday at an all-inclusive Roman caravan park in the south of France. They were greeted on arrival by the Green skirts.

'Here's the key to your caravan,' said the receptionist. 'Your camp fire is located to the right of your caravan and has a spit for feasting, your latrine is located to the left, and your drinking water can be obtained at the Roman bath house, which I strongly suggest you all visit as soon as possible,' said the receptionist as she placed her hand over here nose.

'You will find your entertainment passes in your pack, which entitle you to free use of the theme park, including full mega challenge, Velcro Olympics, double-lane bungi run, diddy man football, and the eliminator. All children should be accompanied by an adult. Your passes also entitle you to free access to the amphitheatre.'

'We have had enough of them to last a lifetime,' Gladigator interrupts.

'Finally, for your evening's entertainment, you are entitled to free entry to Cesar's palace. You are advised to take your seats early, as the bingo starts at 7 p.m. sharp.'

'The bingo!' Ram Ses shouts with a glint in his eye.

'Just ignore him,' said Billy the kid. 'Can I go to the theme park?'

'Yes,' said the receptionist, 'just as long as you are accompanied by an adult.'

In the background the Peacocks can be heard arguing with the attendants who were loading the luggage onto a cart to take to the caravan.

'That's our job,' said Peacock Senior.

'I will have my union on to you,' replied the attendant. 'Now get lost.'

Suddenly Gladesgator stops the conversation with a deafening scream. 'Right you lot!' she shouts. 'I am here for a holiday. You two Peacocks are now free, therefore stop trying to do everyone's job. Now I am off to the baths to get pampered.'

The rest of the party heads off to the theme park. The Agitators and Billy the kid are having a ball. Ram Ses is in his element counting all the kids, and Harry the horse is almost drinking the local pond dry. The Peacocks are going around conducting safety checks on the theme toys and enjoying arguing with the attendant's shop stewards. Harry the horse comes dashing up from the pound. 'You will never guess who I just bumped in to,' says Harry, excitedly.

'Who?' asks Gladigator.

'Steve the stallion,' he replied.

Everyone started to laugh.

'What's he doing now?' asked Big Scot.

'He pulls the luggage carts to the caravans,' said Harry. 'He can't keep the smile off his face. He just kept repeating, "Who said working for the council was boring now?".'

'Good for him,' replied Gladigator.

'Can we all go and get ready for Cesar's palace?' Scot the giraffe interrupts. 'I am getting fed up with all these kids sliding down my neck.' The party left the Peacocks and the kids to get on with it and made their way back to the caravan.

Night fall has arrived and everyone has settled down after a good feast and starts to make their way to the glittering Cesar's palace. Just as they reach the entrance, a whispering sound catches Harry's attention from the bushes, 'Over here, Harry.'

The Agitators drives the horseless chariot into the Auchinlea pond

He approaches the bushes and finds Steve the stallion, who says, 'I have some bad news for you. The emperor has commissioned an army to re-capture Gladigator.'

'How do you know this?' asked Harry.

'It's the talk of all the horses pulling the new caravans that have just arrived.'

'Thanks, Steve, I will pass this on.'

Harry informs Gladigator of the news just as he is about to enter the palace.

'The emperor would not do that!' Gladigator insisted. 'He made a promise to all the children of Rome.'

'Yes, but a rematch with you and Tyrannous would bring in a fortune.'

'Okay, Harry, let the others know, but don't say a word to Gladesgator, just in case this is all only horse talk.'

They all enter the palace and Gladesgator is handed the programme for the night's entertainment. 'Gladigator, they have acrobats, jugglers, and spear throwers with audience participation,' she says. 'They also have singers and, oh no!' she says. Gladesgator lets out a scream as she enters the main hall – the compare is the handsome Marc Anthony.

At that moment you could hear a pin drop, as thousands of eyes turned round, staring at the new arrivals.

'Do you mind?' asked the Green skirt. 'The bingo has just started.'

'Err, sorry about that,' said Gladigator, to silent giggles from the Agitators.

'Over here,' whispers Ram Ses. 'I have kept you all a seat.'

'Move your head,' someone shouts out to Big Scot the giraffe. 'We can't see the numbers.'

'If you can see the numbers, then why do we need to be quiet?' Scot replied.

'What was the last number?' shouts Ram Ses. "I only need one more,' he says in a panic.

'Lost count again?' asked Scot.

'Can't you sit at the back?' says Ram Ses.

'I am going up to the souvenir shop,' he replies, and off he went. Scot is standing at the back of the queue, towering above everyone, and he can see the sales girl struggling at the counter – it is Shazza the squirrel. 'OK, line up! Line up!' she shouts. 'Two for the price of one; or twenty-five percent off for a single pair. Get the latest underpants from Brittany, guaranteed to keep you warm under your battle dress.'

'Why are they called undergarments?' shouts one of the Romans.

'They are called underpants,' Shazza replies to loud sniggers.

'Why are they not called overpants?' asked someone in the crowd. 'If you wear them under your pants, no one will see them.'

'No, you don't understand,' said Shazza.

Big Scot cuts in on the conversation, 'All right, all right, you lot, enough! Give the girl a break, at least she is trying,'

As the crowd disperses, Scot asks Shazza if she would like to go for a popcorn. She agrees and puts the closed sign on the counter.

'What is your name?' she asked.

'I am Scot.'

'You are Scot?' she asked with a confused look.

'That's right, just Scot. I am not George or Jerry, just plane Big Scot, okay? Do you have a problem with that?'

'No, not at all,' said Shazza.

The night moves on and the two Peacocks are talking to Fraser the falcon. He had just come off stage, where he was part of the magician's act, flying from under his cloak at the end of the performance.

'That must be a boring job, having to do the same thing every night?' asked Peacock Senior.

'It's all right; I have had worse,' said Fraser. 'You see, I used to be a scout for the emperor's army. I would fly on ahead and report back on the enemy positions. However, since the empire has invaded everyone, there are no wars left to fight.'

'No one left to fight?' says Peacock Junior.

'Well, there is some work at the top of Brittany, but they are building a wall and even closing that down. No, it's all gone now,' said Fraser, 'unless we enter a recession and people start to invade us.'

Meanwhile, Gladigator was in the games room, participating in the new spear-chucking game called darts. Ram Ses is, of course, keeping the score.

'You need a single seven and double top,' says Ram Ses, as one of Gladigator's spears lands on the wall just above his head.

'Your talking is putting me of,' shouts Gladigator. They are cut off by Gladesgator, 'Come quick, the singers are about to start.'

Back in the main hall they settle into their seats to watch the entertainment. Just then the Agitators interrupt, 'Can we get money for the hamburger stall?'

Gladesgator whips out a ball of wool from her knitting and ties it round their mouths. 'I don't want to hear another word. Now sit down and be quiet. I am on holiday as well, you know.'

The crowd is screaming, 'Entertain us! Entertain us!' Suddenly a fanfare of trumpets sounds out and Marc Anthony makes the introduction: 'Now, fellow Romans, all the way from Brittany we have a new double-act sensation, Clair Voyant and Fitsy Mac Ferret!'

The crowd go wild as they take the stage.

'Hi, folks, my name is Clair Voyant, and I can tell you your future.'

'How can you tell the future?' a voice from the crowd shouts.

'I can talk to the gods,' says Clair Voyant. 'They are beside each and every one of us all the time and in the future as well.'

'In that case, then, are the gods beside me in my caravan?' someone asked from the crowd.

'Well, of course!' replied Claire.

'They can't be,' said the voice, 'it's a tent I am living in.'

Loud hysterical laughter fills the room.

'No, listen to me! Listen!' shouts Clair. 'We will all be reborn again lifetime after lifetime. One day we will all work for a thing called the department, where we will all have different jobs to do. We will all work together as part of a team to try and land something called a plane. We will all have to think outside of the box.'

'Why won't we be able to think inside the box?' asked a member of the crowd.

'Because you won't be able to see the bigger picture,' said Clair.

'Won't they have invented cinemas by then?' someone remarked.

'Yes!' said Claire.

'Don't talk rubbish! Can't you tell us something that we don't know?' shouts a voice. 'That just sounds like working for the council. Is that all we have to look forward to?'

Loud boos ring out amongst the crowd.

'I came here for a holiday, not to be reminded about work.'

The booing in the crowd continues. Suddenly they start chanting. 'Where are the singers? Come on, someone sing us a song. Sing us a song. Sing us a song. Come on, someone sing us a song. Sing us a song. Sing us a song.'

Meanwhile, during the bedlam the emperor's army arrived and are covering all the exits. They are also backstage ready to arrest Gladigator. Marc Anthony informs their commander that this is Cesar's palace, and if you interrupt the performances, you will have the emperor to answer to.

The commander agrees to wait until the end of the night and his men will arrest Gladigator when he comes out. Meanwhile, Marc Anthony returns to the stage. 'Calm down, citizens, at last we have that great singer Fitsy Mac Ferret, with a new song he has written himself.'

Fitsy takes the stage to a deafening silence and starts to sing his latest song. 'Mistral please,' he shouts. The band strikes up and he starts to tap dance and bursts into song. *You have got the sun, so life is sunny, to make it fun, you don't need money.*

The crowd start to boo.

What more do you want. He ends the song with a flick of his top hat and shouts, 'You ain't seen nothing, yet'.

The silence is broken by a lone voice, 'That was rubbish! That song will never be a hit!'

'Yes, it will!' says Clair Voyant.

'Shut it!' shouts the voice. 'Sing us something we know!'

'OK,' says Fitsy. 'Here is a lullaby my old granny used to sing to me when I was a baby.'

'Mistral, please?' Fitsy tilts his hat over his eyes and shrugs his shoulders, beginning to sway from side to side and bursts out into song.

Oh I'm a Roman in the Gloman on the bonnie banks of Clyde… Oh I'm a Roman in the Gloman with a lassie by my side.

A great calm comes over the Roman audience and they all start to close their eyes as Fitsy continues to sing.

That's the place that I like best, oh Roman in the Gloman in the morning.

He finishes the song to the sound of snores. Outside, the emperor's army is sleeping, as they had heard the singing also.

'I think I will call it a night, too,' says Gladesgator. 'Let's all go back to the caravan; it has been a long day.'

Gladigator is met by Harry the horse as he leaves the palace.

'It's true,' he says to Gladigator. 'Take a look around you. It's the emperor's army; they are out for the count.'

'Okay,' says Gladigator. 'Round up everyone; we have to leave now.'

There is a team meeting back at the caravan.

'Where will we go?' asks Big Scot, with Shazza the squirrel sitting on his back.

'We will head for Scotland. They are building a wall there. Once we are over the wall, we are out of the emperor's empire and his reach.'

'The road will be tough and full of danger,' warns Fraser the falcon. 'I will come with you. I can be your eyes and ears.'

'Count us in,' said Fitsy.

'I can tell you what is going to happen,' said Clair Voyant.

'When I need your advice, I will ask for it,' replied Gladigator.

'Is there anyone else with us?' shouts Gladigator.

'Count me in,' said Steve the stallion. 'The council will send me back to Rome after this mess.'

'That's the council for you,' interrupted Harry.

'Okay, let's get organised,' said Gladigator. 'Let's hitch Harry and Steve up to the caravans.' You two Peacocks start to gather the army's weapons and sandals and throw them in the back. Remember to throw in their helmets also.'

'I have spoken to the rest of the caravan drivers and they will come as far as Brittany with us.' said Harry. 'We have to head north and hitch a ride on the ferry to Brittany.'

The Agitators sprung into action, quick as a flash wrapping the wool from Gladesgator's knitting around her mouth. 'The last thing we want is her waking the Romans up or we will never get out of here, Pops,' said Agi. Gladigator nodded in agreement.

So it was that the Gladigators and their ever-growing band of friends cut their holiday short, quietly slipping out of camp. As they moved out, Peacock Junior's voice could be heard whispering in the darkness, 'If I was Gladigator, I would contact the holiday rep and ask for my money back.'

'Shut it, Thomas,' came an even softer whispering reply from Peacock Senior.

CHAPTER 7

The Journey

It is AD 127. They headed north toward the port of Calyx and pretty soon were deep in the heart of what was left of the once mighty empire of Gaul,. which had fallen to Roman rule some 180 years earlier. It was made up of the Helvetia tribes, from what is now known as Switzerland, and the Suevi, another group of tribes from ancient Germany, who had fought over the centuries to control the land now known as France.

Faced with the unprecedented challenge of the ever-growing and all-conquering empire of Rome, the tribes banded together to take on Julius Cesar in what came to be known as the Gallic wars. Cesar, after a four-year battle, eventually defeated the Gallic tribes and won control of the last strong hold of northern France. The final blow had come at Alesia, when Cesar captured the great Vercingetorix, chieftain of the Averni, who had famously led a massive coalition of tribes against the Roman armies. Vercingetorix was taken to Rome and exhibited in Cesar's homecoming victory march as an example. However, this only served to unite the bonds of tribes who had been enemies for centuries. They would continue to fight together for the next few centuries against the common enemy of Rome, mounting a sporadic resistance that would always drive fear into the future occupying Roman armies' hearts. 'I can still recall the day we first encountered the Gauls,' Gladigator reminisced.

'Fraser the falcon is coming in!' shouts Ram Ses.

Gladigator brings the caravans to a halt.

'Roman roadblock up ahead,' says Fraser, as he swoops down to land on Gladigator's shoulder.

'How many?' asks Harry.

'Too many,' came the reply.,

The emperor always had road blocks near to the ports in order to ensure he knew what was going in and out of Brittany and, of course, to impose his taxes and take his share of merchant goods.

'Here is what we will do,' said Gladigator. 'We will send one caravan up front and the guards will take it to the side of the road to search it.' Meanwhile, the rest of us will dash through and make a run for it.'

'What about the caravan left behind?' asked Fraser.

'You let me worry about that,' said Gladigator. 'Send for the Peacocks; let's see if their latest invention works.'

'Okay.' says Peacock Senior, showing Gladigator, 'you pull up the two pins and the caravan should be left behind.'

Gladigator set his plan in motion and sure enough, the first caravan, pulled by Harry the horse, is stopped at the edge of the road, as Steve the stallion and the rest thunder by.

'Rather you than me, Harry,' shouts Steve, as he passes. 'I am out of here!

'I will see you in a minute,' laughs a confidant Harry.

'Halt! Stay where you are, says the guards, as they point their spears.

Suddenly they hear two loud clanging noises as Gladigator pulls out the pins. Harry the horse sprints away, leaving the caravan behind to reveal his splendid chariot, the Rayton Rocket, complete with Gladigator aboard.

The Romans stand gob-smacked on either side of the chariot. In the next instant, two loud ringing sounds are heard as Gladigator hits both of them square on top of their helmets with the two metal pins.

'There's the bell, Harry,' shouts Gladigator. 'And we're off!' says Harry. He pulls away in a cloud of dust as the two Romans' armour continues to shake. It was there on that spot the world's first convertible transport was born.

As they thunder up the road, Gladigator can see the rest of the party up ahead.

'Slow down, Harry, there is something wrong,' he cries.

'Oh no!' says Harry. 'It's a Roman foot patrol.'

In the distance the two Peacocks are standing on top of the caravan arguing as Bible Billy the kid is frantically gum slinging with both barrels. Gladesgator is screaming in full flow and the centurions are holding their ears. The Agitators, taking advantage of her distraction, are dashing in and out, swiping their legs as they go. Gladigator can see the commander on horseback racing toward the group.

'Hit it Harry!' he shouts.

The chariot and the horseman come together and Gladigator reaches out grabbing the horse's reins at the side of its mouth, twisting it down to the ground as he passes. The commander flies straight through the air, landing on top of Gladesgator.

'Thank god,' says one of the centurions, 'I thought she would never shut up.'

Just then thunderous noises are heard coming from the woods and a whole army of little Gauls appear and overrun the Romans. The foot patrol takes flight and heads into the woods to flee the Gauls.

'Are you not going to give chase?' shouts Ram Ses.

'Not at all,' came the reply. 'Just watch this.'

Suddenly the air is filled with scream after scream that seemed to last forever, coming from the dense wood.

'Ah, that would be John the giant,' says the little voice.

Gladigator and his friends all draw a mighty breath as the screams are replaced by the rustle of the bushes as someone came toward them.

'I don't like this. Get ready, Harry, this guy must be massive.' says Gladigator.

Suddenly John the giant appears in front of them and they all let out a sigh of relief.

'Giant? I mean giant?' says Big Scot the Giraffe. 'How tall are you?'

'I am almost 6 feet.'

'What? And you are John the giant?'

'That's right,' said John. 'The name is not George or Jerry, just plain John, do you have a problem with that?'

'No, not at all,' said Scot. 'That's cool by me. I fully understand.'

As the roars of laughter die down, the elder of the tribe comes forward. 'I am the general,' he boldly announces with his chest in the air, his chin held up, supporting a beard that hung almost to his knees. 'General de Gaul, leader of the resistance. Welcome to France. And who might you be?'

'I am Gladigator.'

'Gladigator of Rome, who defeated the emperor's mighty Tyrannous in the Circus Maximus?'

'That's the one!' shouts Harry.

Great cheers echoes down the tribe, whilst they throw their hats in the air.

'We knew you were coming this way, as the word on the street was that the Romans had been briefed to be on the lookout for you,' said the general.

'Can I ask you,' said Gladigator, 'What is the story with John the giant?'

'Well, he is a giant to us. We are all only four feet tall,' said the general.

'No, that is not what I meant. How could he defeat an entire Roman foot patrol single-handedly?'

'Oh, that's an easy one. Come and see.'

Both parties enter the woods. There, amongst the trees, are all the Romans hanging upside down from ropes around their ankles.

'We set traps with ropes and counterweights,' said the general.

'Counterweights?' asked Ram Ses. 'What calculation did you work out in relation to the fulcrum and the maximum distance load?'

'We set many traps close together to shorten the fulcrum and maximise the retraction.'

Suddenly Ram Ses lets out a scream as he is lifted into the air.

'Yes, just like that,' said the general.

Gladigator lets out a roar. 'Can we cut out the science lesson? You are confusing my two Peacocks!' he shouts.

'Incidentally, can I borrow one of your Peacocks?' asked the general.

Gladigator nods.

'On you go, Thomas,' says Peacock Senior.

'But Dad.'

'Don't argue, Thomas. Off you go with the nice little Gaul.'

Junior makes his way into the thicker woods with the Gauls.

'Do you have any news about what we face at the port of Calyx?' enquired Gladigator.

'That is what we are about to find out,' replied the general.

Just at that they are interrupted by the sound of the Romans laughing hysterically from the bushes.

'What's going on?' asked Gladigator.

'We are interrogating them,' said the general.

'Come with me; they should be about to talk.'

There, deeper in the bushes, the Gauls have taken off the Romans' sandals and are tickling their feet with Peacock feathers that they had plucked from Peacock Junior.

'Dad! Look what they did to me!'

'Calm down, Thomas. They will grow in again. Whilst we are at it, cover up! Have you no decency, man?'

'I think he needed a new coat, anyway,' said Bible Billy.

'Are you ready to talk?' the general asked the Roman commander.

'No!' said the commander.

'Do you want me to send for Scot the giraffe?'

'Ah ha ha ha,' even more hysterical laughter echoes out. 'You mean George the giraffe, don't you?'

'Very well, then,' said the general. 'I will send for John the giant.'

'Ah ha ha ha. No, please, enough, enough, we will talk, we will talk,' says the commander. 'I can't take any more.'

'Then speak, man,' said Gladigator.

'There will be little resistance at the port, but once you are out to sea, a Roman warship with full battle ram awaits off the shore of Britannia.'

'We will set out for the port at night fall,' said the general. 'We will see you safely on board, but once you are at sea, you are on your own.'

'We have a deal,' says Gladigator.

'What do you want us to do about this lot?'

'Oh, don't worry about them, I will take care of that,' said Gladigator. 'Fitsy Mac Ferret, show yourself.'

Fitsy and Clair Voyant stepped out from the bushes.

'You will all soon be going for a nice sleep,' says Clair.

'I doubt it,' said the commander, 'hanging upside down like this.'

'Trust me,' she smiled.

'Fitsy, do your stuff,' shouts Gladigator.

Oh, I'm a Roman in the Gloman with a lassie by my side; I'm a Roman in the Gloman on the bonnie banks of Clyde.

'Amazing!' says the general.

'I know, and it works every time,' replied Gladigator, as they both walk away to the sound of loud snores echoing in the background.

Night falls as they march into Calyx. The port is bustling and the markets lining the harbour are doing a roaring trade. 'Duty free. Get your duty free. All goods smuggled past the Roman road block untaxed by the emperor. Get your original Peacock feathered jackets! Get your feathered jackets here,' shouts the voices.

'How much for the jacket?' asked Peacock Senior.

'I see you must have bought one last year,' says the stall holder. 'You look like you could do with a new one.'

'No, it's not for me, it's for him,' says Peacock Senior, as he points to Junior.

'One piece of silver,' said the stall holder.

'Why don't you sell me two for the price of one?' said Shazza the squirrel. 'I will then sell you one back for one piece of silver.'

'But I won't have made any money.'

'No, but you won't have lost any either, and you will have one less jacket to sell and you can go home quicker,' argued Shazza.

'Well, it is a foul night. Okay, you have a deal,' came the reply.

'Run that one by me again?' says Ram Ses.

'Shut it,' Junior shouts, as Shazza throws him the jacket.

Gladigator buys up all the Roman candles at one stall and heads for the terminal.

'One drachma per person, three per chariot, and four for caravans, please,' says the girl at the desk. 'Thank you very much. Here are your boarding passes. Have a nice cruise.'

Gladigator gathers everyone together before boarding. 'We will have to take over the ship before we reach Britannia, before the Roman warship intercepts us,' he explains.

'But none of us know how to sail a ship,' said Ram Ses.

'Well, we will have to learn as we go along, as we have no choice in the matter,' says Harry.

'Thank you for choosing your trip with Galleon,' the young hostess said as the party approached the ship. 'May I have your boarding passes, please? Parking bay is ahead for caravans and chariots. Follow the staircase to the middle deck for your conveyances, and the feasting room is on the upper level, but no children are allowed in that area. Your journey will last approximately two hours.'

'What's on the bottom deck?' asked Agi.

'Errr, the bottom deck?' said the hostess. 'Why that is the rowing room, where the driver and the slaves are that power the ship.'

'Can we see the slaves, Dad? Can we? Can we?' asked an excited Tator.

'Well, that room is normally out of bounds, but I am sure if I have a word with the slave driver, he may make an exception for two little friends,' the hostess suggested.

'Oh, yippee!' cried the Agitators.

Gladigator smiled and thanked the hostess.

'If you give me a minute, I will arrange things,' said the hostess, and off she went.

'Okay,' said Gladigator to the Peacocks. 'You two survey where the crew is. When I release the slaves, show them where the crew is and grab the ship.'

'Yoo hoo, boys. You may go in now. The driver will see you,' cried the hostess.

'Okay lads, you know what to do,' said Gladigator.

'Sure thing, Pops.'

The Agitators entered the rowing room, a cramped, damp, and dimly lit place. The smell of sweat filled the air from the labour of the malnourished slaves. They were seated in two rows of forty, chains round their ankles, which were covered in sores. If the ship were to sink, they would all drown, as their chains were bolted to the floor. Behind them stood the slave driver, ladle in hand, drinking from the water barrel, tormenting the thirsty slaves. No one looked round or dropped their rowing pace for fear of the slave driver's whip on their back.

'Ah, come in my little friends,' said the slave driver as he walked toward them down the aisle. He was a large, pot-bellied figure with a bald, shaved head. He shook their hands and turned to walk away.

'You have to enjoy pain to do my job,' he said.

At that moment the Agitators swiped his legs from under him at lightning speed. Down he went.

'Pops! Pops!' shouts Agi.

Gladigator comes barging in, knocking the door off its hinges. He picks up the long whip and ties the slave driver's hands behind his back with it, shoving him face down on the floor as he places a foot on his back.

'Listen to me! Do you all wish to be free men?'

'Water!' someone shouts.

The Agitators start to distribute the water, going down the lines with the ladles.

'Does anyone know how to sail a ship?'

'We are all Greek sailors,' came a voice. 'We were captured in one of the naval battles during the Roman–Merthradates war.'

'Who might you be, sailor?'

'I am Admiral Hector.'

'Admiral?' shouts Gladigator.

Gladigator instructs everyone to stretch out their chains and stand back. He runs down the aisle, smashing through the chains one-by-one with his sword, freeing the slaves. Once again they are back to being sailors.

'Listen up! A Roman warship awaits us at the shores of Britannia. Now go and prepare the ship for battle.'

The sailors take over the ship as Gladigator consults the admiral up on deck.

'Have you any idea what you are taking on?' said the Admiral.

'Not a clue; that is why I would treasure your advice.'

The admiral began to talk as Gladigator listened intently. 'She will most likely be a Liburnia class cruiser. She will be eighty oars in strength, carrying fifty marines for boarding, who are skilled in hand-to-hand and close quarters combat. They will also have a corvus.'

'What is that?' asked Gladigator.

'It is a boarding device, like a draw bridge, with two metal spikes that are designed to pierce and lock onto the other ship. If the sea is rough, they won't use it for fear of capsizing; however, if it is calm, they will. They will have little blow pipes with small arrows dipped in tar and set alight and they will pepper the hull of the ship as they draw close. They also may decide to ram us, however they will have to drop their sails for that.'

'Can I borrow the long centre chains that you were all bound to?' asked Gladigator.

'What on earth for?' asked the admiral.

'Come with me; I will explain when I address the men.'

'Here is my plan,' said Gladigator as they walked away.

Two hours later the galleon is approaching the shores of Britannia. The ship is in darkness following the admiral's recommendation to stay undetected for as long as possible. The sea is calm, and for the first time that night the clouds clear, allowing a bright moon to shine down. There in the darkness is the faint outline of the Roman warship at anchor.

'They will see us as we get closer,' said the admiral.

'It's okay,' said Gladigator.

'Remember,' he said to Bible Billy, 'you await my signal, when you see their masts fall.'

'Okay,' said Billy.

'Now hand over your gum.'

'What? All of it?'

'Yes, all of it,' said Gladigator.

He, together with Gladesgator and the Agitators, then slipped over the side of the ship into the still calm waters, hauling the giant chains behind them. Ten minutes later they arrive alongside the warship. As the slaves slept, the Gladigator wound the chains around the large oars, binding them all together. The Agitators then walked along the oars pushing the gum into the protruding blow pipes.

'Let's see them fire their little flames now,' said Agi.

They all stood up on the oars and pulled themselves up onto the deck. A guard spots Gladesgator's hand on the edge of the bow. He looks over and she pulls him behind her, head first into the ocean. The Agitators slipped down the stairs and tied up the sleeping slave driver. Gladigator entered the room and smashed all their chains free.

'Who are you?' he asks.

'We are the druids of Britannia,' came the reply.

'I am going to sink this ship. Can you all swim to shore?' Gladigator said.

'Yes,' came the reply.

Suddenly the master of arms shouts out and awakens the ship. 'Galleon approaching! Galleon approaching!'

The Roman marines all jump to their station. They arm their blow pipes by pulling the flaming arrow back only to discover their hands are stuck and on fire. They are running about the deck as Gladigator arrives up top. The marines rush him, but he chops through the mast and it falls, covering them with sails.

At that moment, having seen the agreed upon signal, Bible Billy takes out his sling and starts slinging Roman candles toward the warship.

The deck is burning all around as Gladigator lowers the one ton boarding ramp, causing the ship to list to the side. As Gladigator walks to the end of the ramp and starts jumping up and down, rocking the ship, the slaves dive overboard and head for the shore. All of the Roman marines regrouped and walked toward Gladigator, causing the ship to list even further to the side.

'Not too far,' said Gladigator. 'You will topple us. Everyone stay perfectly still.'

Just then the master of arms comes to the front with his arms around Agi and Tator's necks.

'If you care for them, you will come to me, Gladigator.'

'I hope you can swim,' replied Gladigator, 'because the Agitators can.'

With that he gave a mighty jump on the end of the boarding ramp and the ship began to roll over on its side. The marines are caught up in the rigging and their screams can be heard in the dark night as the ship slowly rolls over, belly up.

A few moments later the Gladigators surface and start swimming toward the galleon. Once they are safely back on board, to a round of cheers, the admiral advises Gladigator, 'We can't enter Dover, they will be waiting for us.'

'It is okay, we will go ashore in Cornwall. Our new friends, the druids, will be waiting for us at the shore.'

'This is an incredible story, Gladigator. I am just going to check on Dan and Blondie for a second. I will be right back,' said Alex.

'I will come with you,' said Gladigator.

They leave the Auchinlea sports base, but there is no sign of the car. As they follow the tyre treads, Alex and Gladigator walk down to the pond and they can see the car sitting on the small island in the middle of the pond. Alex picks up his mobile and dials the AA.

'Hello!' says the operator. 'Can I have your membership number?'

'Yes,' says Alex, '7814392.'

'Yes, I have your account records here. How can I help?' says the operator.

'You will never believe this,' says Alex.

'Yes, I will,' said the operator. 'According to our records, your wife has written off your last two cars.'

'No, even still, this one you won't believe.'

As Alex explains, the Agitators and Dan and Blondie hide behind a smiling Gladigator.

'Oh well!' says Alex. 'They won't be here for another hour. We might as well go back to the sports base and you can continue your story.'

New found friends Dan the man and Agi head back to
the Auchinlea sport base

CHAPTER 8

The Enlightenment

Everyone returned to the sports base and the Ricky-canos occupied the Agitators by taking them into the Gladiator gym and showing them how to work the fitness machines. Alex continued to listen as Gladigator took up the story.

After disposing of the Roman warship they swung around to the coast and picked up the druid slaves. As they headed for the Devonshire coast, the druids told the story of how their land had fallen some sixty years earlier and how the druid god Merlin had changed their Queen Bodicea into a gator so that she would be disguised and not be captured, nor made an example of in Rome, the same way the Romans had shamed Vercingetorix, the chieftain of the Gauls a few years earlier.

She was turned into a gator as there would be no wild animal in Britannia that could attack her and she would be able to defend herself. Gators were also known to live for up to one hundred years, therefore she would have plenty of time to wait it out, as she could not be changed back until after the Romans left. However, mystery still surrounds the queen, as she was never seen again.

Gladesgator stepped forward and announced, 'I am your queen; I am Bodicea.'

'But you can't be,' said the astonished slaves.

'I assure you I am,' said Gladesgator.

'How did you manage to unite the druids to fight the might of Rome?' asked one of the slaves.

'After my husband died, I was told that no one would ever fight led by a woman. I called the tribesmen's bluff. I told them, "You may have the strength of men, but I have the courage of a woman." They had no choice but to fight or their reputations would have been in tatters to let a woman fight alone. I developed a mighty scream that could be heard across the battlefield, driving fear into the Romans and courage into the druids.'

She then explained how the travelling circus was hunting for wolves to take back to Rome for the Coliseum. They were gob smacked to discover a gator in Britannia.

'They had dammed up a stream that I was sleeping in and threw a net over me. They then tied up my mouth and legs. I was then taken to Rome. I was in a circus pen, awaiting transport to the Coliseum, when I managed to escape. I hid on the side of the road watching for chariots to go by. I had led the druid army against Rome on my chariot and learned my skills from an early age; I was confident that I could make it back to my homeland if I could capture one. I finally spotted a chariot after waiting two days, and I dropped down from a ridge, landing in the chariot, knocking the Roman clean off. I grabbed the reins and headed for home.

'Ten seconds later, someone had put a wooden ramp on the road covered in leaves, and the chariot was propelled up in the air and I fell to the ground. By the time I stood up, Gladigator was standing beside the chariot, holding the horse's reins. "What do you think you are doing stealing my chariot?" I asked. "Your chariot?" said Gladigator. "Your chariot with these Roman markings?" "Yes, well, I borrowed it," I said. "More like you stole it," said Gladigator. I started to shout and he started to shake, and the rest was history from there. It was love at first bite and he somehow persuaded me to come to his master's training camp. There would be three square meals a day, and a good chariot driver would teach the young Gladiators. After all, what did I have to go home for – I would just be hunted by the Romans in Britannia the same as in Italy. At least I would have some sort of life there. We were married in the training camp and our children were born in the training camp. We had a relatively peaceful life until the whole of Rome went mad for the amphitheatre grand prix. Tell me is Merlin still alive?' asked Gladesgator.

'Why of course, he is a god!' came the reply.

The druids agreed to take them to meet Merlin at his roundhouse at Stonehenge. We travelled through the forests and arrived several days later. The roundhouse was deep in a forest clearing and was as big as a modern-day circus tent. It had a stone fire in the middle and a gap at the top of the roof to let out the smoke. The elders were sitting around the fire enjoying a feast when they entered. Merlin recognised Gladesgator right away.

'It is our Queen Bodicea!' he announced to gasps from the elders. 'Your majesty, you have returned to lead us against the Romans! I shall prepare a potion to restore you to your former self.'

'No!' said Gladesgator, just as Gladigator and the Agitators entered the house. 'This is my family now,' she announced, as the elders gasped. 'This is my husband, Gladigator.'

'The Gladigator who defeated Tyrannous?' asked Merlin.

'Yes,' came the reply.

'You are in great danger!' said Merlin. 'The gods informed me years ago that Tyrannous and his Gladiators made a pact with the devil. All the children over the ages will be in danger of his evil.'

'We know,' said Gladesgator. 'The children of the future have to be protected. Gladigator is the children's champion of this age, therefore he has to be the champion of all ages.

'I will prepare a potion that allows you to live through the ages,' said Merlin.

'No!' said Gladigator. 'I will eventually grow old and Tyrannous would defeat me.'

Merlin paused for a moment, then replied, 'Not if I were to freeze your age in time. Then you would not grow old.'

'I do not want to live forever,' said Gladigator.

'No, you won't. You will still be mortal, however, unless you meet with an accident or are defeated in battle, you will not age.'

'What about my family?'

'They can drink the potion as well,' said Merlin, 'but they will always be children, their ages will be frozen.'

The Gladigators retired to one of the surrounding huts as Merlin prepared the potion.

Some hours later, Merlin entered the hut. 'I have prepared everything, but before you drink, I must tell you all something,' Merlin insisted.

He began to speak, 'There are many mysteries in life, but none more mysterious than life itself. The body may die, but the spirit lives on. All of us have lived many times and will live many more times. The process is called reincarnation. All the potion is going to do is trap you in the same body until you or fate chooses to move on. You can do this because your soul belongs to you. However, in Tyrannous' case, his soul belongs to the devil. He believes that the devil will give him a honoured place once his two-thousand–year-old pact has ended. However, no one should ever trust the devil.'

'Most people live their lives going from reincarnation to reincarnation, never knowing who they really were or currently are. Who are you, Gladigator?' asked Merlin.

'My parents roamed the jungles of Africa. I was captured when I was a baby and grew up in the circus,' said Gladigator.

'How old are you Gladigator?'

'I don't know,' came the reply.

'You think you know yourself, said Merlin, 'but you don't.'

'What are you telling me, old man?'

'I knew your father,' said Merlin.

'What? You knew my father? Speak!' roared Gladigator.

'Your father is none other than Vercingertorix, the high chieftain of the Gauls.'

'No! You are wrong, you are wrong!' said Gladigator.

'I assure you that I am right. I helped prepare the potion for you.'

'What potion? Speak, old man.'

'When your father was captured, the Gauls prayed to the gods to protect you so that you would one day be able to lead them like your father. There was a fear that you could become easy prey for Tyrannous; he would have known instantly that you would grow up to be a great warrior. The time was AD 55, six years before we made a similar potion for our Queen Bodicea. It is true you were captured by the circus—'

'But,' interrupted Gladigator, 'I was human?'

'Yes, you were.' replied Merlin. 'In my time, I have taken many forms, I have been a stag and a cat and an owl. The forms we take in future lives is not important, it is the soul that counts. You will eventually want to move on, as the soul needs this. The potion will give you all a gift that you will be able to pass onto someone, the ultimate gift of your body, frozen in time. However, you will not be able to pass it on unless you meet a similar soul to yourself that is worthy of the gift. If you perish in battle, the gift perishes with you. You must win in battle in order to protect the gift and pass it on.'

'Why was I not informed before of my father? I would have slain many more Romans,' said Gladigator.

'You were a vulnerable child. You are the protector of children – you could not grow up having hate in your heart. The children of the Circus Maximus and Rome idolise you for this. In the battle for good and evil, you could not have defeated Tyrannous and the devil without these qualities,' answered Merlin. 'If you allow hatred into your heart now, evil will befall the children of the world for generations to come. You will forfeit your right to be the children's champion. Look at your sons, would you like them to grow up to hate?' asked Merlin. 'Of course you wouldn't. You must use your powers sparingly, saving them for the day of the final reckoning, the day you rid the world of Tyrannous. After that, you can pass your gift on any time.'

'Where will I go if I pass on the gift?' asked Gladigator.

'Have a look at the northern lights when you get to Scotland. That is where the gods of the Celts and the Gauls feast and dance. Only they can decide where your soul goes next, but if you trust in good, then evil can never follow you.'

At that point Merlin left the hut. Gladigator and Glades cuddled up. 'We must give our sons the biggest drink,' said Glades. 'I would not want to outlive them.

Gladigator and his family drink the potion

Gladigator agreed. They woke the Agitators and forced them to drink from the chalice while they were still half asleep. They then held each other's hand and swiftly drank the remainder of the potion between them.

The next morning they awoke to news from the camp that the Romans were searching all the woods looking for Gladigator after the news spread regarding the sinking of the Roman warship. Gladigator approached Merlin.

'It is not safe for my family here, I must get beyond the wall to Scotland. I must get out of the empire's reach.'

'I know,' said Merlin. 'I knew you were going to Scotland last night. Remember? The northern lights?'

'How did you know?' asked Gladigator.

'Because it is fated,' answered Merlin. 'My men will escort you as far as Cumbria. However, there is no way of predicting where the Romans will strike.'

'Yes, there is,' said Fraser the falcon. 'I have friends in Britannia. Leave it to me.' And off he went.

'Are you finished?' asked Harry the horse. 'You have spent the night listening to the old one talking a load of bull, while we are out here worrying when the Romans will strike next.'

'We will be leaving soon,' said Gladigator.

'Well, you better get a grip on Clair Voyant. She is over there talking to Merlin, and once those two get started, we will never get away.'

Just then they are interrupted by one of the tribesmen. 'Master Merlin, come quick! We have brought you a magnificent round table washed up from the Roman warship.'

'A round table?' said Gladesgator. 'What on earth will you do with that?'

'Ah,' said Merlin, 'that is my next big adventure. You are about to start out on yours. Like I said, life goes on.'

With that they wished Merlin well and the party broke camp and continued their journey.

'Round table?' said Harry. 'I think the old guy is round the bend.'

'Shut it, Harry,' said the two Peacocks as they disappeared into the forest.

CHAPTER 9

The Battle of Hadrian's Wall

The Gladigator crew, backed up by the Greek sailors, were guided by the druids through thick forest after forest, and swampland after swampland, keeping them hidden until they reached the lake districts of Cumbria. Upon arriving in Cumbria, they made a clearing in the dense forest. It would be here that they would prepare themselves for the fight ahead. They intended to burst through Hadrian's Wall at the Roman fort of Trimontium, known today as Newstead, near to the border town of Montrose on the other side of the wall.

This part of the wall ran through the three large Eildon hills, hence the name 'Tri'-montium. Hadrian's Wall ran for eighty miles from the east coast to the west coast of Britannia, and took eight years to construct. Along its perimeter were garrisons every few miles, with a series of forts between them. Small towns, acting as trading posts, were popular around the garrisons and forts. The Romans constructed roads that would allow access for supplies for the soldiers who guarded the walls, with each garrison responsible for patrolling a length of the wall.

Hadrian's Wall was not the first or only wall of its time. History tells us of the great Antonine wall built further north, designed to keep out the dreaded Pics, or Caledonians. However, the vast terrain made it impossible for the Antonine wall to be built from coast to coast, as natural barriers such as hills and dense forest created gaps. The native marauders were knowledgeable, and exploited these gaps, forcing the Romans to retreat back some years later to the flatter lands to achieve their objective of a wall linking up completely, coast to coast. The wall was also backed up by fifteen–feet-wide trenches all the way along its front, and garrisons were built on higher hill points.

The Greek sailors were masters of building war machines, and in no time at all, Admiral Hector, backed up by Ram Ses doing the calculations, set about building giant catapults on wheels, known to the Greeks as ballistas. They consisted of large leavers trusted by large, coiled springs, courtesy of the Peacocks, made by melting down some of the Roman armour they had recovered from previous excursions. The machine was bound by straps woven from thin strips of bark. They would form strong binding once wrapped round the wood and left to dry out in the sun. These ballistas were capable of firing large boulders at a force capable of penetrating enemy walls. They could also fire boulders dipped in pitch and set alight to become flying balls of flame. There was no shortage of volunteers to command these new machines. However, Bible

Billy the kid managed to persuade them that he was the man for the job.

They also built large crossbows, called scorpios, which fired a large arrow pulled back by a large strap. They also built battering rams on wheels from mighty oaks, with wicker roofs to protect them from the arrows that would rain down from the walls above. They would have an advantage in the fact that they were trying to burst through the wall and out of the empire; it was on the other side of the wall the trenches had been dug to keep the Caledonians from getting in. The Roman army's main defensive forces would be patrolling on the perimeter of the outside of the wall as no attacking forces were expected from behind the wall.

Meanwhile, Fraser the falcon, true to his word, had been busy seeking out his friends. He flew toward the cliffs of Wigtownshire. Below him in the distance he can see hundreds of thousands of seagulls and herring birds sitting in rows and rows on cliff edges and small island rocks protruding from the coast. His radar is picking up faint signals from the ground as flocks of birds take off and land, patrolling their island coast and looking for prey. In the noise from below, he can hear a voice, 'This is Tracey, your ground controller, can you identify yourself?'

'Fraser the falcon, seeking permission to land,' he replies.

'Can you state the nature of your business?' came the reply from Tracey.

'This is Fraser the falcon seeking a meeting with Stephen the squadron leader.'

'You are free to descend,' said Tracey.

As Fraser comes in, he can see the geese and swans that use Wigtownshire's cliffs as a staging post for their winter migration. This was as busy as the modern-day Glasgow airport. The bustling noise grew louder and louder as Fraser came in to land.

'Anything to declare?' asked a voice.

'Nothing,' said Fraser, 'as I will be travelling inland and not abroad.'

'State the nature of your business.'

'I have come to meet with Stephen the squadron leader,' said Fraser.

'One moment and I will contact him on the radar,' said the voice.

A few minutes later, Stephen the squadron leader flew in, accompanied by his two wing commanders, Ewan and Jimi. 'How are you Fraser?' asked Stephen, as he comes in to land.

'Who is he, Pops?' ask Ewan and Jimi as they land.

'This is Fraser the falcon, a veteran of aerial recognisance in many wars,' said Stephen. 'Fraser, please meet my two sons, Ewan and Jimi.'

'Together we are the Wing Bandits,' said Ewan.

'What gives?' asked Stephen.

'I need your help,' replied Fraser. 'I am flying for Gladigator against the Romans and we are launching an attack on Hadrian's Wall,'

'You mean Gladigator that defeated Tyrannous?' asked Stephen.

'Yes, it is he,' said Fraser.

'What do you need from us?' replied Stephen.

'We need aerial cover on the wall. We hope to link up with Gilber and the Caledonians. I need to get a message to Gilber in his hillside fort so he can launch an attack from the other side of the wall at the same time as Gladigator. That is the plan,' said Fraser, 'to catch the Romans in the crossfire and defeat them in the confusion.'

'Where are you intending to strike?' asked Stephen.

'We plan to hit them at Trimontium,' said Fraser.

'Trimontium? You realise that Governor Weir is in charge of that garrison?'

'Who is he?'

'He is more known for his battle tactics than his fighting skills. He is a very clever adversary. His troops will be well organised, and his scouts are second to none. He will already know that Gladigator is coming and will know all his strengths and weaknesses.'

'That is why we need the help of the Caledonians,' said Fraser.

'Leave everything to me. The Romans have been raiding our cliffs and stealing our eggs. I don't think I will have too many problems in securing the help of the herrings to launch an attack on the wall. I have a plan that I am sure Gilber can help me with. Do you have a date for the attack?' he asked.

'Yes,' said Fraser. 'One month from today.'

'Go to Gladigator and tell him the attack will start with the Caledonians from the north side of the wall. He must wait and then be prepared to pounce.'

'Roger that,' said Fraser.

'Who is Roger?' asked Ewan.

'Apologies,' said Stephen, 'as you can see, my sons are still learning.'

'In that case,' said Fraser, 'over and out, as I must return to give Gladigator the news.'

'True to his word, squadron leader Stephen contacted Gilber.

The mighty Roman empire was stopped in its tracks. They had conquered all of Europe and all of Africa. They had defeated famous armies, including Hannibal, over the years. Many wondered why the Romans feared the Caledonians and Gilber; why had Hadrian been so desperate to build the wall? What was it about tiny Scotland and the Caledonians that they so feared. One advantage that Scotland had was its small mountains and peaks, over three hundred, known today as the Munroes. However, its strength was in the hills, thousands of them. The ancient Caledonians built their forts on top of these hills. They would farm in the valleys, but slept in the hillside forts, surrounded by moats dug out below.

Another advantage was their fighting technique. They would fight in small packs, descending from their mountain forts in darkness and attacking Roman foot patrols. As swiftly as they came, they would retreat back up the hills to their forts in the darkness of night. When the Romans would attempt to attack these forts, mustering armies to climb the natural hills, their heavy armour would exhaust them by the time they got to the top of the hill, making them easy pickings for the Caledonians, who were armed with nothing other than a sword and dressed in cloth. The Caledonians could hold off the Romans for months in their hillside forts.

The Romans would lay siege to them, attempting to starve them out for months on end. However, this took up a lot of the army's manpower. Furthermore, whilst their attention was focused on starving one particular fort out, the other forts would take advantage and create havoc with the Roman garrisons down in the valleys.

The Caledonian's tactics of hit and run were the first steps to modern day guerilla warfare; swooping down from the hills, hiding in the dense forests, their knowledge of their own terrain giving them stealth-type powers. The enemy cannot conquer what they cannot see. The mere mention of Caledonia drove fear into the ordinary Roman centurion's heart. If you were posted to Caledonia, more often than not, you had let someone down or were being sent as a punishment.

Another advantage was the fact that Scotland was thousands of miles away from Rome and the empire's supplies. There was not an abundance of replacements for the Roman army that could be readily available in the matter of a few weeks.

All the small hillside forts were generally local families that would give birth a few hundred years later to the clan system in Scotland. These were the days when Scotland was united. In future centuries, the nation would allow itself to be divided through greed and a thirst for lands and individual power, a division fuelled by invading English armies centuries later. History would prove that Scotland could never be conquered by anyone other than itself. But all that was to come. This was now, in the age when Scotland stood united, led by Gilber.

One month later, the great day approaches. It is a Friday and the monthly pay day up on the Roman wall. The Roman soldiers are cueing and in a good mood, dreaming of the feasting they would do with their pays. In amongst the rabble at the front of the queue is Carol the counter, the chief administrator to the governor. She is dealing with the usual disputes.

'But I done fourteen foot patrols this month, why am I short?'

'Because you wore out a pair of standard issue sandals which had to be replaced. They have to be transported all the way from Rome and that costs money,' said Carol.

'But four days' wages? I will have my union on you.'

'Go get your union,' said Carol. 'What about the person that makes the sandals and the people who have to transport them? Are they not to be paid? I wonder what your union would say to that?'

'I have lost half a day for a spear sharpener,' said another soldier. 'Why would my spear need sharpened if I did not throw it this month?'

'You took part in quelling an uprising with the locals, did you not?' asked Carol.

'Yes, but—'

'You claimed your bonus money, did you not?'

'Yes, but I never personally threw my spear.'

'So you admit it,' said Carol.

'Admit what?' said the soldier.

'That you made a false claim. Fill in the claim form and I will send it to the governor.'

'No, no, it's all right. He will send me on foot patrol against the Caledonians.'

'But then you will earn more bonus money,' said Carol to the shaking centurion.

'It's okay,' came the reply. 'Honestly, it's okay.'

Suddenly the queue is disrupted by the sound of the alarm trumpet and all the centurions rush to their positions on the wall.

On the north side of the wall, the Caledonians send a token party to the gate of the great wall at Trimontium.

'Someone approaches, governor,' says a centurions guarding the wall. Governor Weir watches as the two figures approach, until they are below him, stand two little figures just over three feet tall under a white flag.

'Speak!' shouts Governor Weir.

'Surrender now and you and your men shall be spared,' says the voice.

'Who might you be?' replied Governor Weir in the midst of hilarious laughter from his soldiers peppering the wall.

'I am Lorraine the liberator,' says the small figure.

Once again hysterical laughter echoes round the walls.

'Where is your army? asks Governor Weir.

'That is not important right now, however, I have brought their great leader as proof of my intent.'

'Who is this great leader that stands before me?' asks the governor.

'I'm Mcquader the invader,' came the reply, greeted almost instantaneously with even louder laughter from the guards on the wall.

'Who are you going to invade?' asked the governor.

'I intend to drive the Roman Empire out of Britannia and back across the sea to Gaul,' came the reply, followed by roars of laughter that could probably be heard in Gaul.

'How will you govern this land that you have conquered?'

'That is not for me to decide, I am a warrior. Once the battle is over, it is up to others to govern.'

'Who shall govern then?' asked the governor.

'I shall,' said Lorraine the liberator.

'But how will you pay for this new empire?'

'I shall raise taxes throughout the land.'

'Do you have any experience in tax returns? Do you know the paperwork involved in running a treasury? The VAT returns alone could take up a lot of your time. Then there is the problem of tracking down non-payers that will cost you more money. You will have the unions to deal with, and just when you think everything is going well they will go on strike. Do you have pension funds in place, in order that you can bring an army out of retirement to run the key services during any disputes?'

Lorraine the liberator places her hand on her chin. 'You know I never really thought about it like that. Can we retire for today so that I can have a think about this and we can come back and invade you tomorrow?'

'Take all the time in the world,' said Governor Weir, to deafening laughter all around.

'Thank you,' said Lorraine the liberator as she returned to the forest, leaving Mcquader the invader to stand alone.

'As for you,' said Governor Weir, 'you can take that look off your face,'

'What look?' asked a confused Mcquader.

'That menacing look, that's what look,' said the governor.

As Mcquader attempted to change his natural look it became even worse, much to the amusement of the Romans on the wall.

'I shall remember you mocking me when I look down on you with my sword,' said Mcquader in his best, squeaky voice, as he turned and fell over his own cloak, receiving much laughter from the centurions. Off he went into the dark bushes.

'Someone on chariot approaches the south wall, governor,' shouts the guard.

'What now?' says the governor.

'It is Gladigator, sir! He approaches.'

'Gladigator?' shouts Governor Weir. 'Are you sure? Okay men, you all know what to do, we have prepared for this.'

Gladigator draws up on his chariot as Harry the horse brings them to a halt. 'You there on the wall,' he shouts.

'Governor Weir!' came the reply.

'I wish to pass peacefully into Caledonia. Please open your gates and I will be on my way.'

'I am under the emperor's orders to send you back to Rome, Gladigator, therefore you shall not pass.'

'Okay, have it your way,' says Gladigator. He turns and lets out a loud shout, 'Send for Gladesgator!'

Gladesgator pulls up in her chariot pulled by Steve the stallion to an "oohing" sound from the Romans on the wall. She lets out a deafening shriek. 'Now open those gates and let us through, or I will scream and scream,' she shouts.

Instead of holding their ears, the Romans on the wall fall about laughing.

Gladigator looks down to a confused Harry the horse and shrugs his shoulders.

'Very well,' he shouts, 'I can easily send for Scot the giraffe and John the giant.'

'You are having a joke. You mean George the giraffe and Jerry the giant?' came the shouts.

'Very well,' said Gladigator. 'Have it your own way. Send for Fitsy Mac Ferret,' he shouts.

Fitsy runs out to the front of the wall and is greeted by the legions bursting into song to taunt him.

Come on, Fitsy, sing us a song, sing us a song. Come on Fitsy, sing us a song, Fitsy, sing us a song.

'Okay,' says Fitsy, 'you asked for it.'

'Give them both barrels!' shouts Harry.

I'm a Roman in the Gloman on the bonnie banks of Clyde, I'm a Roman in the Gloman with a lassie by my side.

All around the wall can be heard the side-splitting laughter of the Roman centurions. Fitsy looks around to Gladigator. 'I don't understand it,' he says.

Meanwhile, up on the wall, Governor Weir turns to one of his commanders and says, 'It was a smart move to invest in those ear plugs for the guards. Look at them! Gladigator is dumbfounded!'

However, this was to be the governor's undoing – it was because of the ear plugs that his soldiers could not hear Gilber and the Caledonians attacking from the north side of the wall.

'Keep it going,' said Gladigator to Fitsy.

Oh I'm a Roman in the Gloman in the morning.

Unknown to the Romans, Fitsy's singing was serving as an inspiration to the Caledonians attacking from the north side of the wall. Suddenly the Roman laughter is shattered by the crash of a fire ball on the end of a metal chain that had been hurled crashing into the wall behind them.

'Action stations! Man your posts!' shouts the governor, as the centurions turn to face the invaders on the other side of the wall. There, from the dense forest, stood Gilber, all seven feet of him, with a Celtic swagger, and dressed in a plain black cloth kilt and sheepskin jacket. He carried a wicker-woven shield that was woven into a protruding circle, making spears hard to land, as they skim off the shield. It was also lighter than the Roman shields, giving him more speed in battle.

The Caledonians were driving crude chariots that are light-weight and mobile on the battlefield. The chariots would drop off warrior passengers, armed with spears and axes, then double back to pick up more warriors and bring them to the front of the battle. They would then pick up the first lot of warriors and wisk them away from the battle. This continuous replacement of warriors insured that those fighting on the front line never tired whilst the enemy eventually would tire. This light-weight flexibility allowed for a continuance onslaught by the Caledonians.

However, the Romans had not built an empire and won victories over the centuries against the world's best armies for nothing. They were precision fighters, taught to fight as a group and not as individuals. They would fight in triple lines, with the front line being continually re-enforced by the second line to fill in the gaps at the front created by those who had fallen. The last line would bring continuous supplies of weapons to the front and fill in for the second line. Meanwhile, the front line would cleverly use their shields to form a tortoise defence, the soldiers at the front joining their shields together to form a wall and the soldiers behind them holding their shields above them, creating a shell that was impregnable to the enemy. As the tireless tactics of the Caledonians pounded away on the Roman front line, the shell-like defences insured the Romans suffered few casualties. Something had to give and it did.

Suddenly, on the south side of the wall, Gladigator's forces attacked, forcing the Romans to fight on both sides of the wall. Bible Billy gave the order to release the catapults, sending flaming rocks hurling toward the walls. Some passed over the wall, landing on the Roman tortoise formations, forcing them to scatter and be run down by the Caledonian chariots. Scot the giraffe was frantically re-cocking the catapults as the Peacocks reloaded. The Greeks were also firing their crossbows, knocking the Romans off the walls. Meanwhile, Gladigator was leading the battering ram against the wall doors.

High above them the garrison is in flames. Gladigator's forces ram the doors open and he climbs the stairs to the top of the wall. He is met by the governor's commanders. As he fends them off, the governor runs to attack Gladigator from behind, but he is intercepted by Mcquader the invader, who jumps down on top of him from one of the Caledonian sage towers.

'Where is Gilber?' asks Gladigator.

'He is down below, fighting the legion,' comes the reply.

Gladigator looks down and sees the Roman tortoise formation open up. He knew from his time in the Coliseum and the Circus Maximus that this was an old trick. They would allow the enemy to charge through their ranks, then close the gap, isolating them from their comrades; others from behind would finish the trapped enemy off. He sees Gilber enter the trap.

'No!' shouts Gladigator to Gilber, but it is too late. The ranks close and Gilber is trapped. Gladigator, quick as a flash, takes a run at the sedge tower, rocking it forward. As it topples to the ground, Gladigator holds on as it topples, splitting the Roman line. Gladigator flings himself into the Roman tortoise formation, knocking many to the ground. When he stands up, he and Gilber are fighting back to back.

In the background, the Gladigator forces have come through the gate of the wall and are engaging the Romans from behind, whilst the Caledonians engage from the front. However, Gladigator and Gilber are still trapped in the Romans' tortoise formation. Suddenly the formation is burst clean open with the arrival of Harry the horse and Steve the stallion, pulling their unmanned chariots. Gladigator and Gilber jump on board as the formation scatters to be ran into the ground by the Caledonians.

Eventually Gladigator's forces and the Caledonians meet in the middle as the remaining Romans retreat to the wall.

'Pleased to meet you,' said Gladigator to Gilber.

'Your reputation precedes you,' came the reply, 'but we have a big problem now.'

Gladigator turns to see the remaining Roman legion, three hundred deep, form a massive tortoise formation and slowly advance toward them. The Caledonian chariots are whizzing all around the formation without penetrating them.

'Where do we go from here?' says Gladigator.

'Don't worry,' says Gilber. He gives a deafening blow on his horn and the skies start to fill. Fraser the falcon picks up a distinct voice on his radar.

'This is squadron leader Stephen, are you reading me? Over.'

'Yes,' says Fraser, 'loud and clear.'

'Please ask your forces to retreat to the forest,' says the squadron leader, 'to prepare for midge bomb attack.'

'Midge bomb attack! What is that?' asks Gladigator.

'Welcome to Scotland, the home of the humble midge. Just think of them as little piranha fish with wings guaranteed to bite through anything. We prepared hundreds of branches with little pouches filled with swamp water, and where there is swamp water, there are midges.'

'Okay,' said squadron leader, 'we are going in.'

'Here come the wing bandits!' said Ewan and Jimi. 'Midge bombs away!'

Suddenly the Roman formation starts to throw their armour to the ground, rolling about, scratching under the bombardment. The Caledonian and Gladigator forces surround them, grabbing all their weapons. They are left standing in their long-johns, scratching away, as is the governor as he gives the signal to surrender as Mcquader the invader stands on his chest, pointing his sword down at him. Hereafter history would proclaim the great victory over the Romans by the Caledonians at Trimontium.

However, now that Gladigator had managed to escape the Roman empire, he asked Gilber to ensure there was no mention of him or his men in the battle. Gilber understood and agreed, as Gladigator did not wish for his whereabouts to get back to Tyrannous. As for Governor Weir, legend has it that, faced with the shame of defeat, he could not go back to Rome and had to flee the empire. It is told that he fled to just outside Paisley, where he taught the locals irrigation and how to build waterways; a town still exists named after one of his old bridges, known as the Bridge of Weir.

As Gladigator's forces headed for the west of Scotland, a little voice could be heard shouting in the middle of the Roman prisoners, who were still scratching themselves from the midge bits. 'Underpants! Yes, underpants. Get the latest undergarment from the continent. Two for the price of one. Line up, line up!'

'I told you there was money to be made from these,' said Shazza to a smiling Scot.

CHAPTER 10

The Fun Factory

At this point, Gladigator's story was interrupted by the Ricky-canos and the Agitators entering the office. 'Quiet down there,' said Alex.

'So what happened after Hadrian's Wall?' asked Alex.

'Well, we were all free men. Some settled down along the journey, others came here, to what you now know as Glasgow, with us.'

'Where are they now?' asked Alex.

'They, of course, all passed on. However, like Merlin said, life changes. I am sure, if I looked hard enough, they will still be around, only may have been reincarnated into other forms. I know quite a few had said they would like to try being human; others did not have that fascination. The Peacocks still roamed the gardens of Provan Hall house right up to the beginning of the last century. Then they suddenly left.'

'So, you settled down in Auchinlea and have been here ever since,' said Alex.

'Yes, well, err, sort of,' replied Gladigator.

'No, we lived in the Bishoploch first, said Tator.

'Hush!' interrupted Gladigator. 'Yes, well, we lived in the Bishoploch for a while then decided to move downstream of the Molindiner to the Auchinlea.'

'What? The Molindiner passed through Auchinlea?' asked Alex.

'You are standing on it. The stream is under this building as we speak. It used to run into the old Monklands canal, which was built in 1790 to follow its path,'

'The canal?' asked Blondie.

'Yes!' said Agi. 'In 1769 the magistrates in Glasgow had to find a way to transport coal from the east to the centre of Glasgow. They commissioned James Watt, who invented the steam engine, to build a waterway.'

'A waterway?' said Blondie. 'Just like a motorway today?'

'Well, yes, if you like,' said Gladigator. 'It opened in 1790. In 1807, passengers were ferried along the canal in boats drawn by horses. Strange thing was they always called their horses Harry or Steve. It was used to ship coal on barges from Monklands to Glasgow. At its peak around 1865, thousands of workers lived and worked on the canal.'

'So, this was a busy place back then?'

'Yes, absolutely. We used to swim in the canal and then open the goodie boxes,' said Tator.

'What were those?' asked Blondie.

'They were the cargo that had been lost overboard from time to time,' answered Gladigator. 'You never knew what you would find.'

'Were you ever spotted by the locals?'

'The children on the boats used to laugh and wave to us, but their mothers, sitting under their little umbrellas in their long, thick dresses, used to shout, "Really children, don't be silly." I never understood that,' said Agi. 'We were in the water to cool off; they were the silly ones sitting in their long, heavy dresses in the sun.'

'You must have been there throughout Scottish history. The Agitators told us you met Mary, Queen of Scots,' said Dan the man.

'Yes,' replied the Gladigator. 'She lived in the Provan Hall house for a while. One of the Baillies, Sir William, was a close friend of hers. She stayed there while her husband was ill in St Nicolas hospital at the Provan lordship.'

'What about William Wallace?'

'I never met him, but his army often passed through. He was captured by the English further up the Molindiner at Rob Royston.'

'Wow!' said Blondie.

'What was the housing estate like?' asked Dan.

'There was no housing estate, but there were lots of farms. A lot of the streets in Easterhouse take their names from the farms, such as Wellhouse, Avenue end, Netherhouse, Rogerfield, Greenwells, Commonhead, Queenslie, Provanhall, Lochwood, and Blackfriars. There was even a farm called Easterhouse.'

'You must know everything, Gladigator,' said Dan. 'True or false? Does the loch ness monster exist?'

'I don't know,' said Gladigator. 'I do recall that Big Scot the giraffe and Shazza told me that Scot was there swimming with his long neck sticking out of the loch and there were hundreds of locals sitting on the bank shouting "monster, monster" at him. They eventually moved on because they could not get peace, but I am told Shazza made a fortune selling mythical stories about the loch to the visitors, or should I say the early monster hunters. She had the gift that the monster would always appear just when she was doing one of her famous tours. Big Scot was not too pleased. He said he caught pneumonia on several occasions, especially in the winter.'

'Wow!' said Dan.

'What about the old man of Hoy?' asked Blondie.

'I am older than him,' laughed Gladigator.

'What about Tyrannous?' interrupted Alex, quick as a flash, as if to catch Gladigator by surprise.

'Oh. err. he is still trapped in the African mines, as far as I know,' Gladigator replied in a hesitant voice.

'Do you think he will ever get out?' asked Alex.

'I hope not!' said Gladigator.

'Anyway, he has still got to find me,' he continued, drawing the Agitators a glancing stare.

'Anyway, enough about us,' said Gladigator. 'What about your dad?'

'What about me?' asked Alex. 'Don't expect me to follow you. I am just an ordinary guy with an ordinary story.'

'We used to read about your weightlifting exploits,' said Agi.

'Read them where?' asked Alex.

'When the drunks used to throw their fish suppers away in the park at night, we used to read about you in the greasy newspaper.'

'What? My dad was in a fish supper?' asked Blondie.

'No, Squeaky, he wasn't actually in the fish supper.'

'Shut it, Blondie,' said Dan the man as he placed his hand across his little brother's mouth.

'I don't know really why it was,' said Alex, 'but I was born into the new housing estate in 1960. This was heaven for my parents, who had grown up in the slums of the inner city – all the fresh air and modern houses. However, for us kids, there were no community facilities. I was even late in starting school as we had to wait until they were built. That was when the gangs were formed, in the early years of the estate, out of boredom. Years later, the invisible or mystical boundaries between territories have stayed with us. I suppose you could say the gangs were tribal, just like the Gauls and the druids, or the Caledonians. There was never anything exciting to do. We used to play in the old canal before they built the motorway on it when I was a boy; it was quit dangerous. However, we did have some excitement in the sixties when the famous singer Frankie Vaughan came to Easterhouse to campaign for youth facilities for us. He was young enough to steal your mum, and old enough to steal your granny, too.'

'Would he have stolen Lizzy doll?' asked Dan the man.

'No, somehow I don't think so,' said Alex. 'Anyway, Frankie achieved a lot, but there was a lot of bad publicity came out of it, fuelled by jealous people who tried to twist everything Frankie tried to do to help.'

'Ah ha ha, steal the Lizzy doll,' interrupted Blondie.

'Sorry about that,' said Alex to the Gladigator. 'He does that sometimes.'

'I suppose I kind of grew up with a chip on my shoulder, wanting to show the world that just because I came from Easterhouse did not mean I could not do well at something. I suppose that's where the weightlifting came in. It did not really matter what you were good at, but coming from this neighbourhood, it was important that you were good at something. Which I was, and arrogant with it to.'

'In what way?' asked Tator.

'I would tell people I was going to win before the competition started.'

'Just like Claire Voyant?' asked Agi.

'Yes, that's right, sort of.' said Alex.

'Was the chip on your shoulder from the fish supper, Dad?' joked Dan the man.

'I enjoyed the competitions most probably the way you enjoyed your many battles down the ages.'

'Ah ha ha, from the fish suppers,' interrupted Blondie.

'Like I said before, he does that sometimes,' explained Alex.,

'Pretty soon I had others training under me and produced many champions from the area and from across all the so-called gang areas. It was good for the community as we were generating a massive amount of media and television coverage over the following years, competing at Commonwealth, European, and world championships. Suddenly I realized the fact that the success of the club was showing the community in a better light. I had read about the mythical Gladiators of Rome, and I don't know why I hit on the idea to call the programme after them, but something was drawing me to the name. I now know why, after you've told me about what happened at the quarry.'

'We had to get the kids fit to compete in later years; that is why we devised the play programme. Soon the kids were not just participating in weightlifting, but all sports. I realized that if kids can have the opportunities I did not have in my early years, they could achieve anything. They look up to the Gladigator mascot. It teaches them to dream. They go on to become better people when they are older if their dreams turn into ambitions. It is all connected. That is why the work that the programme has built up has to be protected for future generations of Glasgow's children. That is why we are fighting to build the Gladigator fun factory in the Auchinlea park. The new Glasgow Fort shopping park will be here for the next hundred years, and the fun factory can make an income from the shoppers' children. We can then use the funds to continue to keep the children out of trouble and pay for all their future dreams and ambitions. The Auchinlea park is the perfect place to build the fun factory. I know from my personal experience that there has never been any bother with the local gangs in the park, and only recently it was deemed to be Scotland's most child-friendly park.'

'There is a reason for that,' said Gladigator. 'All the youths in the gangs used to be brought to the park by their parents. The parents could not see the Gladigators, but the children could, and they would play with the Agitators. However, once they grew older and their minds became complicated, they would forget about the Gladigators, but we were still there, hidden in the back of their minds. That is why, as youths, they respected the park and there was no fighting. That is also why, years later, when they became parents, they would bring their own children to the park. They would pretend it was because their parents brought them in the past, but in the back of their minds, they knew why they really came to Auchinlea.'

'So that's the magic of Auchinlea?' said Alex.

'Yes, and that magic increased with the Gladiator programme and your Gladigator mascots. It allowed the adults to see,' said Gladigator. 'This is why we must fight to build the Gladigator fun factory, to take the magic of Auchinlea and turn it into the legend of Auchinlea, a place where children dream and a place where adults remember their childhood.'

'We have raised half the funds,' said Alex. 'But there is still a long way to go. Just like back in the sixties with Frankie, there are those who don't dream, those who can't see what the fun factory would mean to the children.'

'We will help you,' said the Gladigator.

'How can you help?' asked Alex.

'We can create re-enactments of my chariot races in the Circus Maximus. I will train your staff up with wooden sticks to fight like the real Gladiators of old.'

'My staff can't see you.'

'No, but I will train you up to teach them. Your programmer, Marc, can add the re-enactments into your gala days across the city. I will come and take part; the people will think I am another mascot.'

'You know, you have really got me going here,' said Alex.

'Listen to yourself. You expect the children to believe, but you have to be convinced yourself.'

'Okay, I am in,' said Alex.

Suddenly there is a knock on the sports base door and Alex goes out to answer it. It is the AA patrol man.

'That your car back of the island on the pond? You are lucky it is only two feet deep or we would not have been able to drive it out. A couple of young kids said they saw what happened and were claiming they had seen other kids driving it with two lizards with long tails. They have probably been out walking their dogs and decided to jump in the car for a laugh. That should teach you to keep your doors locked and your car keys in your pocket from now on.'

'Thanks a lot,' said Alex. 'You know, I just did not think as I was only jumping into the building for a second to pick something up.'

'These things happen,' said the AA man, 'but this is one I won't forget.' And off he went.

'We have to get going, Gladigator,' said Alex, 'as we have spent most of the day here and Lizzy doll will be expecting us. I will meet up with you every Sunday at the sports base and you can teach me the skills of the Gladiators. It will be wooden weapons, right?'

'Right!' said Gladigator.

'Okay,' said Alex.

They departed as night fell and the Gladigators disappeared into the park in the glare of the headlights as Alex and the boys drove off. The following week and for a few months thereafter, Gladigator, true to his word, taught Alex what he knew about the fighting styles of the ancient Gladiators, all the time Alex remembering to keep his car keys in his pocket.

The lessons were intense. Gladigator insisted they had to be real to draw in the crowds at their re-enactments. There was the style of the Myrmillo, or fish fighter, so called because of the logo on his helmet. He fought with a large oblong shield that covered his body from shoulder to calf. It gave great protection, however, the down side was it was difficult to wield about. He would normally be pitted against Thraex, who carried a small, round shield that only protected his torso, or Hoplomachus, who carried an even smaller shield. Both of these guys wore leg protectors that came well above the knees. Fights between these guys were the well protected, versus highly mobile, keeping the crowd in suspense.

Probably the most vulnerable of the Gladiators was the net fighter, Retarius, who had only a shoulder guard on his left arm for protection. Although relatively unprotected, he could move at great speed. He would cast his net over an opponent with one hand and strike low blows with his trident through the net.

He customary fought the heavy armoured sector, who although virtually impregnable, would tire very quickly under the weight of their armour. Finally, there was the Equates, or horseman, who traditionally would dismount to finish an opponent off.

'So you fought these guys?' asked Alex.

'I defeated them all in a day,' said Gladigator. 'I am left-handed, and that gave me a big advantage, as a lot of their defensive strategies were based on fighting other right-handed opponents.'

Over the coming months, it did not go down too well with the Gladiator programme staff as they rehearsed all the moves Gladigator had shown Alex. But they perked up once they got their re-enactment dresses from the manufacturer, and some had their very own favourites and started to develop the feel for it. Sure enough, during that long, hot summer, the re-enactments were introduced at gala events all over the city of Glasgow. They entertained the crowds and the publicity spread like wildfire, the Gladigator winning in the end. They could send a Gladigator with a Gladigator to six different locations a day, or have all six and all the Gladiators fighting together, depending on how much someone was willing to pay, or how big the event was. The Gladiator programme was already popular in all the nurseries and schools in Glasgow, and he was famous amongst kids everywhere, but now he was holding an interest with the adults.

The local radio stations started to take notice, and they would turn up to some of the events to report on some good, honest family fun. Suddenly the Gladigator mascots were being asked to turn up at promotional events and we started to gain service agreements with the local authorities promoting all sorts of child initiatives, from fire safety to road safety, you name it. Everyone had learned that any initiatives that seemed boring to the kids suddenly took on more interest if the Gladigator was delivering it.

While all this was going on, Alex was appearing on a lot of television programs, letting people know that the best thing they could invest in for their community's future was their children, and explaining how their activities could divert them from trouble and open up opportunities at an early age – in short, promoting the dream. The adults believed in soap operas on their televisions, why shouldn't they believe in Gladigator, he was no less real. The Gladiator programme also challenged parliament to stick up for charities and ensure social justice in the business community.

Encouraging more contracts that allowed charities to earn their own income, just like the Gladiator programme, insured that children's activities were in the hands of the local communities. For the Gladiator programme, the future fun factory was the way ahead, and the funds just kept rolling in. Pretty soon everyone was talking about the fun factory, and, more importantly, the legend of Auchinlea Park was beginning to grow.

The local television did a piece on the park having won the most child-friendly award once again.

'What is it,' said the television reporter, 'that makes this park so popular? Why do children appear to their parents to be giggling to themselves and pointing to the Gladigator when he is not even there? There is something nice about this place that the children love, and the parents just have to go with it.'

Pretty soon all the funds were in place and the building phase was started. The fun factory would come in through the trees on the opposite side of the pond from the Provan Hall house and heritage centre.

The Fun Factory Re-enactments

Suddenly, just when everything was going well, the unexpected happened. The pen pushers from the Heritage Trust lodged an objection because building the fun factory required cutting through the trees of the park, even though double the amount cut would be planted at the other end of the park. The media were in an uproar and eventually they had to go to the sheriff court, as the parents and children of Glasgow held their breath. The hearing would be heard by none other than Lord Rayton. The Heritage Trust would be represented by Mr Connolly. The court is called to attention by the clerk to a packed audience and media.

'Please be upstanding for the right honourable Lord Rayton?' he announced.

'Okay.' said Lord Rayton. 'I have a splitting sore head, so make this short and talk English to me, man.'

Mr Connolly explained his case, 'The site is of historical importance, my lord, and the scenery is undisturbed since the ice age.'

'Someone should have told that to the Canon of Provan. He built a house there six hundred years ago, and you built a heritage centre next to it,' said Lord Rayton.

'Yes, my lord, but the amount of visitors the fun factory would bring could spoil the park.'

'Are you not dependent, Mr Connolly, on the heritage centre attracting visitors?' replied Lord Rayton.

'The removal of the trees causes some concern.'

'From what I have read in the report, those trees were planted in the mid-1950s; the ancient trees are up near the house. Besides, they are more dried up bushes than trees,' countered Lord Rayton.

'My lord, the park was halved in size when they built the Glasgow Fort park. Are we to lose more of the natural environment?' replied Mr Connolly.

'Why did you build a heritage centre then, if you were that concerned about losing more space?' replied Lord Rayton. 'Is that your case, Mr Connolly?'

'Let's hear the defendants.' said Lord Rayton.

Alex presented his case. 'My lord, the fun factory, it is true, will bring more visitors to the park. You cannot teach children history if they don't visit in the first place. Why was the heritage centre built? Was it only to teach adults? Surely the most important people to teach are children?

'School visits are planned for the heritage centre. The history lesson is more attractive if the children are visiting the fun factory for lunch and to unwind. Blending heritage with leisure is not unknown in Great Britain and has been proven to work. With regard to the Glasgow Fort shopping park, we will increase its visitors through the parents. With regard to the Gladiator charity, we are not beggars, but we reserve the right to piggy back on the Glasgow Fort shopping park's economy for the good of the local community and the children of Glasgow.'

'Do you have anything to add in your summary, Mr Connolly?' asked Lord Rayton.

'Yes, my lord, you have to start to think outside the box. You have to try and land that plane. We all have to pull in the same direction. I mean, Gladigator's mere children's fiction, and we can't put that in front of heritage.'

Suddenly loud snores are heard across the court.

'My lord,' said Mr Connolly, 'please wake up.'

'What?' said Lord Rayton. 'Are you finished? Very well, I am calling for a recess until I make my decision. This court is adjourned.'

In his chambers, Lord Rayton is sitting at his desk when he receives a call from his son. 'Hi, Dad. I have a very excited young granddaughter of yours on the phone.'

'Hi, Milly darling, how are you today?'

'Grand Dad! Gladigator was at my nursery today showing us all how to dance, and he says he will come back and teach me some more! I got a huge cuddle from him, and I told him he has big teeth and a long nose the same as yours Grand Dad!'

'Listen, darling, I have to go now, but you have a nice day,' said Lord Rayton.

'The court is now in session,' shouts the clerk. 'All upstanding for Lord Rayton?'

'Be seated everyone, and I will give you my decision.'

'Can you stand up, Mr Connolly? You say Gladigator is not real. It may not be real to you, but it is real to many young children, bringing them happiness. What parent would not want their child to be happy?'

'But your honour, Gladigator is not real,' said Mr Connolly.

'Shut up and don't interrupt me again,' said Lord Rayton. 'Legends down the years, and indeed historians, even the Bible tell of lizard people throughout history; some called them dragons. For instance, St George, the patron saint of England, reputedly slayed the dragon. If it was not true, then why did the church make him a saint? St Nicolas is the patron saint of children. Who says so? The church does. Santa Claus represents St Nicolas. We adults may not believe in Santa Claus, but we did when we were young, and we also encourage our own kids to believe. We do this because Santa is based on St Nicolas, which we know to be a historical fact. Therefore, why can't Gladigator be based on historical fact with regard to lizard people and dragons? Another example, one that is fundamentally embedded in the Glasgow coat of arms, is Saint Stef, who brought the robin back to life, most commonly referred to as the bird that never flew. Was this fictional? No, it is documented. However, whether you choose to believe it or not is up to the individual, but they cannot dictate their views or opinions on others. Furthermore, what is real and not real in this modern age? We have grown adults watching and believing characters in soap operas. I know, just ask my wife. All I get to watch is the news.'

Laughter breaks out around the court. 'Silence!' says the clerk.

'It would appear as if adults believe that is alright,' said Lord Rayton, 'but children believe that is not alright unless it is convenient for us adults.'

'With regard to thinking outside the box, I think we should put a lid on the box if it is full of people who think like you Mr Connolly. Why anyone would want to land a plane in a children's park is beyond me.Finally, if we all pulled in the same direction, we would all end up on our backsides in the Auchinlea pond. In the interests of children everywhere, I am dismissing your case. There will be a fun factory in Auchinlea.'

The cheers echoed through the courtroom and the media went into a frenzy.

Just over a year later, the fun factory was complete and the whole of Glasgow awaited its opening. There were plans for a massive re-enactment of the Gladiators down in the park prior to the grand opening. Strangely, the pond had been drained to make way for a new fountain to be installed, and it looked just like the Circus Maximus with all the families sitting on the hills looking down in the summer sun.

Crowds looked down from the heritage centre on one side, and the fun factory pavilion on the other side. The stage was set for a fantastic day the whole of Glasgow would enjoy, and the local radio stations and television crews would be out in force to witness it. The Gladiator programme staff were going through their final preparations for the opening, and the Pincocks were washing all of the balls in the play frame, all ten thousand of them! It seemed nothing could go wrong on a day like this. Though it was not known at the time, the legend of Auchinlea was about to reach a new high.

CHAPTER 11

The Re-emergence

A little known, but thought to be mythical, fact about the Wellhouse area of Easterhouse was that it was said to take its name from an ancient well. Some say the first settlers that farmed in the area watered their crops from it. Thereafter it had somehow fallen in on itself or been mysteriously boarded up and forgotten. No one knew where exactly it was, and it was reported to be a matter of opinion. Those who said it lay in the grounds of the old chapel that had burned down a few years earlier would have been right. The area was now cleared and the top soil had been disturbed. It was thought that the well originated by a flaw on the clay bed that eroded the top soil and allowed the water to surface. Through the centuries, the locals would have deepened the shaft to draw more water, but it may have dried up as the clay bed closed in on itself again.

Of course, the clay bed would have been pretty thin at that particular point. The wellhouse area was about two miles from the Bishoploch where Tyrannous had been trapped with his Gladiators centuries earlier. It had been a case of 'oh so close' for Tyrannous and his men, but then again, 'oh so far.' They were nearing the end of their pact with the devil; tomorrow would be the last day and then they would answer to the devil, having never defeated Gladigator or fulfilled their agreement to rain tyranny on the world down through the ages.

Suddenly, as fate would have it, after centuries of searching for an opening, they would find one, in the cold, dark night of Wellhouse. They found what they thought would be their own salvation. There, under a half moon-lit night, Tyrannous and his men slowly emerged from their watery tomb.

'Free at last!' said Tyrannous. 'We don't have much time. We must find Gladigator.'

They sat around the grounds taking in their new environment and planning their next course of action as their clothes dried out.

However, they were in the territory of the so-called *Torrain toi*, the gang of the local, hard men who were ever vigilant with regard to anyone coming through their turf. The Gladiators were about to learn a new language, called fluid Glaswegian, as the local youths approached.

'Haw big man,' said the gang spokesman. 'Whit dae ye think yer dane in our midden? (Why are you in our area?). An wit are ye dane in they daft claze ya pure space cadet.' (Why are you dressed so differently?)

'What language is this?' said Tyrannous. 'I don't understand.'

'I think it is Caledonian, but the tone may have changed over the centuries,' responded. Myrmillo.

'Can you communicate with them?' asked Tyrannous.

'I will try, master.'

'Good evening to you and auch aye the noo,' said Myrmillo.

'Whit do you mean auch aye the noo ya dafty? (Why are you talking like that, you really silly person?) Here big man do you want to gee me a coupler yer skins fur a puff?' (Can I have some cigarette papers for a smoke?)

'What is he saying?' asked Tyrannous.

'I think he wants to smoke your sheep skin jacket, master.'

'Are you skinheads?' said the youth.

'Do our heads look skinned?' asked Myrmillo.

'I have had enough of this,' said Tyrannous, as he grabs the youth by the ear and runs him over to the perimeter fence of the old chapel.

'OH, Haw big chap! Big chap! Cool it man, cool it,' (Oh, the pain!) says the youth, as he winces.

The Gladiators grabbed his friends and hung them up by their jackets on the perimeter fence.

'Don't you know smoking is bad for your health?' said Tyrannous. 'Come to think of it, so are we, if you don't start talking.'

'Please talk slower so that we can understand you,' said Myrmillo.

'Okay, we will,' said the frightened youth.

'That's better,' replied Tyrannous. 'Now where is the Bishoploch from here, we have to find our weapons?'

'Why, that's up at Drummy,' said the youth.

'Is it a defending army playing on their drums to scare people away?' asked Tyrannous.

'No, ya daftey (Don't be stupid.). It is a gang called Drummy.'

'He is doing it again,' said Tyrannous. 'I don't understand? Where is the loch from here?'

'Oh, the loch, you should have said. It is about two miles from here. What kind of weapons are you talking about? Swords, shields, helmets, nets and staffs, do you mean Roman weapons? The ones I read about in the paper the other day?'

'They are ours!' said Tyrannous.

'They are hundreds of years old,' said the youth.

'I know,' roared Tyrannous, 'and they're ours.'

'I don't think this guy is the full shilling,' said the youth to his frightened pals. 'The archaeologists took them to the Kelvin Grove art galleries to exhibit.'

'How do we get there?' asked Tyrannous.

'You will have to get a forty-one bus or three taxis into town. Come with me and I will take you to the main road.'

'Let's move out,' said Tyrannous, and off they went.

Up on the road, the youth flagged down the taxis and the Gladiators and Tyrannous headed for town.

'Where are we off to tonight?' asked a laughing taxi driver.

'The Kelvin Grove art galleries,' replied Tyrannous. 'So that explains the fancy costumes. Good on you, lads, I hope you enjoy your night.'

'The taxis pulled up to the venue and presented their fares.

'We have never paid taxes in our life,' said Tyrannous, 'and we are not going to start now.'

'Be on your way,' he roared.

The taxi drivers were clearly taken aback and radioed in for the police.

'This is as big as the emperor's palace,' said Tyrannous. 'We will have to smash the door in.'

The magnificent Kelvingrove Art gallery

The Gladiators entered the building to the sound of the alarms echoing around them.

'Search the building,' shouts Tyrannous, and the Gladiators spread out.

Two minutes later they regrouped.

'They have animals that don't move, master,' said Thracian.

'That's nothing, they have mummies wrapped in bandages from head to toe,' said Velitus. 'I mean, that's somebody's poor mummy.'

'They have different swords and axes in glass cases with a man in a metal suit inside.'

'See to the man and grab the weapons,' ordered Tyrannous.

'Master, I have found our weapons in the basement. They are in a room called new antiquates, said Secutor.

'Okay, meet me back here in one minute,' said Tyrannous.

Meanwhile, outside the police have arrived. The two young police officers enter the building.

'Come out and show yourself, this is the police,' said the officer in charge.

Suddenly they are brought crashing to the ground by two massive thumps, as they hear the would-be burglars rush past them in the dark and out onto the street. One officer shines his torch on his colleague as he radios in for assistance.

'Hi, sergeant, we are in the Kelvin Grove art galleries. We have just been assaulted by a stuffed baby elephant and a mummy in a big box.'

'Well, arrest the mummy, and I will send for backup,' said the laughing sergeant as he radios back.

Meanwhile, the Gladiators and Tyrannous have just boarded a bus going to Saucheihall Street. Velitus runs up the stairs to be greeted by two youths.

'Hey you,' came the shouts. 'Auld yin!'

'Where do you think you're going dressed like that? Give us your money or your life.' said one of the youths.

Just at that point, the rest of the Gladiators come charging up the stairs.

'I will count to ten,' said Tyrannous.

The youths, shaking with fear, opened the fire exit and dropped out the back end of the bus.

As they are passing through Saucheihall Street, with its Friday night revelers, Tyrannous spots a fast food outlet.

'We must eat to get our strength up to fight the Gladigator.'

They all leave the bus and enter the establishment. Myrmillo orders up the food from the notice board as the rest sit at the tables.

'Can I have a black pudding supper, two Dona kebabs, six fish suppers, one single haggis, two single sausage, and twelve garlic breads?'

Velitus passes the food out as it is being served. The Tyrannous is munching away on his fish supper when he notices through the grease on the newspaper print the image of the Gladigator: "Grand opening of the Gladigator fun factory in Auchinlea park tomorrow at twelve noon".

He can hear Velitus arguing away in the background. "Forty-two pounds is a lot of weight. There is no way all this food weighs that amount.'

'Stop clowning around. You owe me £42,00 for the food. Now pay up,' said Big Annie from Anna's Kebabs.

'It's the Gladigator,' Tyrannous announces, as he picks up one of the tables and throws it through the counter. 'Grab the meat on the spit; we will eat it on the road.'

The Blairtummock House

'This is so unprofessional!' says Big Annie.

Velitus jumps over the counter and removes the kebab rack from the machine and passes it to his colleagues. Tyrannous throws another table through the window and together they all leave through it.

They head down the street past the fancy dress shops. 'Outstanding outfits,' shout someone in the passing crowd.

Just then someone hands Thracian two pound coins. 'I am always happy to help poor students out. I have been there myself, Enjoy the rest of your evening.'

'It's a forty-one bus,' said Tyrannous. 'I remember the youth said that number; it will take us back to the place we came from.

'Yes, master, it says Easterhouse under the number.'

'We must go to this Easterhouse; it mentions that name in the readings of the fish supper about the Gladigator.'

They board the empty bus and hand the driver the two pound coins. 'You students are all the same,' said the bus driver, 'on you come.'

They enter the top deck of the bus to be confronted with a little Glasgow guy sitting on the back seat with his carrier bag, singing away.

I'm Roman in the Gloman on the bonnie banks of Clyde.

'Can you keep it down a bit?' asked Tyrannous.

'Please to meet you,' said the little man. 'My name is Paul Fitzsimons, 'If you give me one of your chips I will take you all to a party.'

'Err, no thanks,' said Tyrannous, 'we all have work to do in the morning.'

As they reached Cranhill, the bus broke down.

'Sorry, lads, you will all have to get off; we have broken down,' said the driver.

'Big chariot not move?'

'No, lads,' laughed the driver, 'big chariot no move. You all have no tickets, therefore you cannot wait for a replacement bus. You will all have to walk.'

'Which direction is Easterhouse?' asked Tyrannous. 'Just follow the Edinburgh road and you will find it a couple of miles ahead.'

During their walk they encountered gang territory after territory of local youths. Police sirens were heard running back and forth to the city centre all night. Finally, they arrived on the grounds of the recently refurbished Blairtummock house, built by the tobacco barons in 1720 as a country retreat. They were less than a mile from Auchinlea.

'This is good enough,' said Tyrannous, 'for tonight. We must be close to Auchinlea. We will search in the morning.'

As they patrolled the perimeter of the grounds, Tyrannous and Velitus looked across the motorway to the landmark floodlit horse of the Glasgow business park that welcomes travelers into Glasgow.

'This is indeed a strange new century,' said Velitus to Tyrannous. 'The people travel in horseless chariots, but yet they still pay homage to the horse.'

'Just as long as it's not Gladigator's horse, Harry; I could not stand that,' said Tyrannous.

They made camp on the bowling green and bedded down for the night. Meanwhile the radio and television stations were issuing news alerts all over the city: 'Police are hunting a group of men thought to be dressed in Roman-style clothes. They are understood to have caused a disturbance in the Kelvin Grove art galleries taking a number of items. They then caused a disturbance in a downtown fast-food restaurant and proceeded to the east end of the city. Police report an unusual surge in gang activities, resulting in a number of people being taken into custody. Once again, sightings of the Roman-style dressed group have been quoted. Police advise the general public to stay indoors and not to approach the group if sighted. Please stay tuned for further bulletins.'

'It's got to be Tyrannous, Dad,' said Dan the man, as they watched the nightly news bulletin on television. 'Remember, his pact with the devil expires tomorrow.'

'But how did he find Gladigator? I have to go speak with him.'

'Be careful, Dad.'

'I will,' said Alex.

'Where are you going at this time of night?' asked Lizzy doll.

'I can't sleep, worrying if everything will be all right for tomorrow's opening of the fun factory. I just want to check a few things.'

'Okay, well, if you must,' says Lizzy doll, 'but don't waken the children when you get back.'

Something played heavily on Alex's mind as he drove to the Auchinlea park. 'Was there something that Gladigator had not told him? Or was this sheer bad luck? He arrived at the car park and pointed his headlights down on to the black darkness of the park. He followed the light of the car down as far as he could into the pitch darkness until it faded behind him and he is left in the middle of the eerie silence of the park.

'Gladigator, we must speak!' he shouted out.

His cry echoed all around the park.

'Gladigator, we must speak,' Alex called again to nothing but silence coming back at him.

He carefully made his way toward the Provan Hall house side of the empty pond, listening for any remote sound that may resemble Gladigator. He cries out once more, but this time he is disturbed by the shattering silence of a lightning bolt striking the Provan Hall wall. It seemed to electrify it. The glare of a magnetic field around the wall lit up the night sky. In his mind Alex could not understand it – how could lightning strike on a clear summer night without rain?

Suddenly, in front of the glare, standing only about ten feet away from him, was the outline of Gladigator walking toward him.

'I know why you have come,' said Gladigator.

'It is Tyrannous, right?' asked Alex.

Gladigator nodded his head

'But how did he get from Africa to here so quick?' asked Alex.

'He was here all along,' replied Gladigator.

'What? Here in Easterhouse? I don't understand.'

Gladigator explained the events of the Bishoploch and the bishop's palace.

'That explain's the weapons that the archaeologists found,' said Alex.

'Yes!' said Gladigator. After I trapped them in the clay bed I threw all their weapons into the loch. I did not think anyone would find them.

'But why did you not tell me about this before?' shouted Alex.

'I was hoping they would remain trapped until their pact with the devil expired. They almost did. I had no intention of alarming you or the boys. However, that is partly why I trained you to train your workers in the art of Gladiator fighting.'

'So the re-enactment was only a cover in case the Tyrannous appeared?' said Alex.

'No, never, I wanted to help raise the funds for the fun factory and we succeeded,' said Gladigator.

'What is that glaring light surrounding the wall?' asked Alex. 'Does it have anything to do with what is going on?'

'It is a transporter light sent down by the gods from the northern lights. When people describe them as the heavenly dancers, what they are actually seeing are transporters coming or going.'

'What is going to happen tomorrow, Gladigator? What match is the Gladiator staff to battle veterans like Tyrannous' men.'

Gladigator just smiled, 'You worry too much.'

'You say the light on the wall is a transporter, but a transporter of what?' asked Alex. 'Souls,' shouted Gladigator, with a roaring laugh that echoed all around the park as he held his arms in the air. 'Souls from down the ages. They are in their own time one second, and the next second they are here.'

Just at that Frazer the falcon lands on Gladigator's shoulders. 'I will scout the area at day break, they can't be far,' said Fraser.

Suddenly, from the glare on the wall, figures start to appear. Noises of voices arguing can be heard.

'Don't argue with me, Thomas. How do I know where we are?'

A thunderous roar is heard as Harry the horse and Steve the stallion come charging up, pulling their chariots behind them. 'This is out of order Gladigator, I was babysitting tonight,' says Harry.

Down of the chariot jumps General de Gaul. 'I brought a few of my friends along. I thought we could set a few traps in the park.'

'Be my guest,' smiled Gladigator.

Admiral Hector came into the company. 'Need a hand with any tactics for tomorrow?' he asked.
Gladigator nodded.

Just then Alex felt a tap on his calf and turned around with the fright of his life. Suddenly he heard a voice and looked down.

'Hi, I am Mcquader the invader, and this is Lorraine the liberator. Pleased to meet you.' said the little voice below him.

'Who's left? Gilber?' says a startled Alex.

'Aye, that would be me, son,' says the massive figure walking toward him.

In the distance they can hear Shazza the squirrel talking excitedly to Scot the giraffe. 'I can't believe it, we are in the age of the global economy,' she cries, 'we will make a fortune.'

'Shush,' came the voice from the tree above. It was squadron leader Stephen. 'Keep it down; you will awaken Ewan and Jimi.'

'Sorry!' said Big Scot.

'So the gangs all here,' says Alex. 'But my guys have to fight with sticks.'

'Not necessarily!' said Gladigator. 'Ram Ses, can you go up to Provan Hall house. Tell the Peacocks to dig behind the red cedar tree. You will find the weapons we took from the Romans.'

'They better all be there,' said Ram Ses. 'I had them all counted; I will know if any is missing.'

'You are going to win, you know, I can tell,' said Claire Voyant, as she pops out of nowhere, with a voice growing louder and louder in the distance behind her. It is Fitsy Mac Ferret.

I'm a Roman in the Gloman with a lassie by my side, I'm a Roman in the Gloman on the bonnie banks of Clyde.

Just at that moment Alex, with all the excitement at the end of a trying day, succumbs and faints. The last thing he hears is the thump of the back of his head hitting the ground, flat on his back.

'Oh look at that,' says Clair, 'he must be descended from the Romans.' Suddenly a streak of gum comes flying through the air, hitting Fitsy Mac Ferret clean in the mouth. Sorry I am late, you all,' says Bible Billy the kid, 'I had a bit of business to attend to. How can I help?'

There they all were, in the pitch black of the Auchinlea night. There would be the final battle between good and evil. The children's champion verses the devil's warriors and their leader Tyrannous. Regardless of whom won, the legend of Auchinlea would be cemented for all time. But would the world remember it for good or for bad? The time had come for the final conflict.

In the whispers of the night could be heard the faint voices of the Peacocks. 'I don't care, Dad, I am not going to sleep with all those Gauls around. It took me three years to grow those feathers back in.'

'Shut it, Thomas,' came the reply.

CHAPTER 12

The Gathering
(The Battle of Auchinlea)

Day breaks and by early morning the park is full of activity for the preparation of the day's eagerly awaited events, a full program of re-enactments, that would culminate in the grand opening of the Gladigator fun factory. Down in the middle of the dried out pond, the Gladiator programme staff are setting up the theme toys and going through their safety checks. Surrounding the pond, the park rangers are setting up the crowd control barriers. The car park attendants are setting up an access zone for the event organizers in readiness for the massive crowds expected.

Of course, all are oblivious to the other late night arrivals from the northern lights also preparing for the event. But those arrivals knew that once the events started they would become visible to the adults, as well as the children, because the adults would believe in the events. Shazza the squirrel is in her element at the shop stall, laying out all the Gladigator memorabilia, ranging from Gladigator wands to Gladigator hats, t-shirts, and, of course, the Gladigator horns. Down in the make-shift pits, the Peacocks are going through the final checks on the Rayton Rocket, with Harry the horse grazing on the grassyslope, looking perfectly calm, along with Scot the giraffe, who was quite at home grazing on the trees, which meant he would not have to bend down. Bible Billy is getting some slinging practice in, while Ram Ses is going through the checklist. Meanwhile, at the other pit stop, Steve the stallion waits for the expected opponents with the Real MacKay. The Gauls are over on the island in the middle of the pond explaining to Gladigator what surprises and traps they had set up for their expected visitors, particularly tthe pulley system they had rigged up, a re-creation of a curvas, the boarding device made famous on the Roman warship, except this one did not just go up and down, but could rotate and swing out from the island and back in again.

Dan the man and Blondie are distributing the programme of today's events on the bleacher seating for the crowds to read later. Down on the staging area, the sound technicians are running checks, testing the microphones on the fifty giant speakers that will address the crowd. Lizzy doll is in the registration tent waiting for the participants in the re-enactment; all have to register and are then given a number and a copy of the rules.

Meanwhile, back at the Blairtummock House, the Tyrannous camp is wakening under the watchful eye of Fraser the falcon.

'Wake up, master, the road with the horseless chariots has filled up, and they are queuing,' said Viletus,

'This is it,' said Tyrannous. 'They must be heading for Auchinlea. They must be going to watch the final conflict. We will follow the queue until we arrive at the venue.'

Tyrannous roused his men and they set off down the lane in the park that followed the edge of the motorway.

Back at Auchinlea, Fraser the falcon swoops in and lands on Gladigator's shoulder.

'They are on their way, Gladigator,' said Fraser. 'We don't have much time.'

'Okay,' said Gladigator, 'we all know what to do, so get ready.'

By this time Tyrannous and his men have reached the traffic lights at the motorway bridge. They are about to cross over the road to the park when they come across Dan the man and Blondie waiting to cross, along with other excited children and their parents.

Tyrannous steps of the curb only to receive a kick on the shin from Dan the man.

'Hey, you big lump, you have to wait for the green, man.'

Tyrannous looks down angrily, then suddenly breaks into a smile.

'The green man? Is that Gladigator?' asked Tyrannous. 'If I wait here, will he come?'

Suddenly he is kicked in the other shin by Blondie. 'No, you fool, Gladigator is in the park.'

A raging Tyrannous grabs Blondie by the neck, but is interrupted by a beeping sound. Suddenly an old granny from the crowd has poked him in the ear with her umbrella.

'Move it, you big clown! Can't you see the lights have changed? You are holding up the queue.'

They cross the road and head into the park. The crowd is filling up and the park rangers meet them at the gate.

'Hello, boys. I like your outfits for the re-enactment. Just follow the signs for the registration tent.'

They make their way to the bottom of the path and are met by Alex.

'Where is Gladigator?' asked Tyrannous.

'All in good time,' said Alex. 'Please follow the path down to the registration tent.'

'This is it,' says Tyrannous. 'Gladigator must be in the tent.'

They start to walk fast, breaking into a jog, then picking up full speed and dashing into the tent armed and ready. Suddenly they are stopped in their tracks by the screeching sound of Lizzy doll.

'Right, you lot, what do you think you are doing?'

The Gladiators all stand rooted to the spot, shaking.

'Err, I do apologise,' said Tyrannous.

Just at that, Velitus whispers in his ear, 'I have never heard such a noise, since the Circus Maximus and Gladesgator.'

'OK, boys, over here,' said Lizzy doll. 'Place your weapons on the table and sign in. Keep a hold of your number that you are given and keep your pass on at all times. A packed lunch will be provided up at the Provan Hall house – do not try to steal an extra one, or you will have me to answer to. Does anyone have any questions?'

'Err, could you be awfully nice and tell us where Gladigator is?'

'It is all in the programme of events. Now register who will be fighting in which re–enactment. Your weapons are being transporteded to the enactment area. Sign the infantry of your equipment and move along, you are holding up the queue, Next, please.'

Tyrannous and his men headed down into the park, passing by the shop stall.

'Get your Gladiator horns, two for a pound, two for a pound,' Shazza shouts.

'I have never seen a squirrel so big,' said Velitus. 'It must be one of those mascots.'

Just at that moment, the Gladiators and Tyrannous jump two feet in the air, shocked by an unexpected earth-moving noise from behind them. It is Dan the man and Blondie.

'Wow, these Gladigator hooters are fantastic!' says Dan, and off they ran.

'It is those kids, again,' says Tyrannous. 'Oh how I hate kids.'

They move on down into the pond area.

'Hi, my name is Alex, and I am your referee for today's proceedings. If you would like to make your way to the holding area on the left-hand side, you can prepare for the events.'

'Where is Gladigator?' asked Tyrannous.

'Oh, he is over on the other side, preparing his team for the fights,' answered Alex.

'Fight?' said Tyrannous. 'So I will get to fight Gladigator?'

'Oh, yes, absolutely, but you will have to wait your turn. There are other events first.'

'I don't mind waiting,' growled Tyrannous, 'just as long as I fight him.'

The crowd is starting to liven up and the children are starting to chant Gladigator's name over and over, much to the annoyance of Tyrannous. Meanwhile, the radio and television reporters are starting their broadcasts.

'Welcome, folks, on this fantastic sunny day in the middle of the splendid surroundings of Auchinlea Park in the city of dreams. We are coming to you live from Glasgow, Scotland. There is a packed audience for a fantastic day of events ahead, culminating with the long-awaited opening of the Gladigator fun factory. The park is amazing – it actually resembles the Circus Maximus of ancient Rome; the drained pond actually looks like an arena. The walkway around it has been widened to look like a race track. The crowd is sitting on the bleacher seating built on the grassy slopes and the noise of the children excitedly chanting away is adding to the atmosphere. I can see the crowds peering down from the heritage centre and others from the fun factory pavilion. Let's go down trackside where my colleague, Mark Anthony, is hoping to catch a word with some of the participants.'

'Thanks for that, Charlie, and I am just going to catch a few words.'

The reporter turns round and catches Tyrannous by the wrist.

'Watch it!' he shouts, as he catches one of his spiked wrist bands.

'Err, hi there,' says the reporter. 'Can you tell the viewers at home and watching across the world how it feels to be taking part in today's re-enactment?'

Tyrannous gives a roar. 'Gladigator will perish this day. Today the world is mine.'

Across the city at police headquarters they are watching the television.

'I don't believe it, sergeant!'

'Believe what?'

'It's that guy, the guy from the Kelvin Grove art galleries.'

'He may work there during the day, but maybe re-enactments are his hobby.'

'No, you don't understand! That's the guy that hit me with the baby elephant!'

Meanwhile, back at the park, 'Well, there we have it, in true warrior style and keeping with the tradition,' said the reporter. 'I am really getting into the spirit too, Gladigator is doomed. You know, Charlie, if I did not know it myself, I would say these guys are playing it for real. Its back over to you, Charlie.'

'Well, thanks for that, Marc. Let's settle back now as it looks as if the action is about to begin.'

The crowd is clapping and the children are letting it rip with the Gladigator hooters as the sound of the commentator's voice rises above them. The commentator begins his announcements:

'Welcome Gladigator fans everywhere. Here is the moment we have been waiting for and the first match up is between the six Gladigator mascots who have each taken a name from the local area against six of the Gladiators. First, to my left, introducing the Gladiator team. Please give a big Glasgow welcome for Essedarius, Retarius, Dimacheerius, Andabatus, Thracian, and, finally, Laquarius.'

They all enter the arena to the crowd booing.

'Now to the Gladigator mascots. I give you Avenue End, Lochwood, Netherhouse, Rodgefield, and finally, bringing up the rear, the mascots from Queenslie and Commonhead.'

They all enter the arena to a massive roar of cheers from the children in the crowd.

'OK, folks, let's explain the first event. There is an opposing team and a large pit facing each other. Each team has to get past each other and make a dash for their weapons, and then its game on.'

Down in the arena, referee Alex Richardson brings the two teams together.

'You will wait for my whistle and break when I tell you. Any last questions? Very well, good luck.'

The whistle blows and both teams crash into one another. The commentator takes over: 'Wow! And there's the scrum as both sides go crashing in. The Gladiators seem to be pushing the mascots nearer and nearer to the pit. Would you believe it? The mascots move to either side and the Gladiators go crashing head first into the pit. The mascots are off and running and on their way, racing to pick up their weapons. Andabatus has made it out of the pit and he is on his way to mount his horse. Meanwhile, the mascots are heading back as the rest of the Gladiators are about to climb out of the pit. Wow! Sensational move from the mascots as they throw their shields like giant Frisbees, knocking the Gladiators clear back into the pit. The crowd is ecstatic, but what's this? It's Andabatus, charging in and out of the mascots with his horse. He runs down one, now two, and another. One of the mascots is heading for the island for cover. The Andabatus is catching up, he is about to strike with his sword into the back of the mascot. Boom! And he is out of there, sports fans, as what can only be described as a boarding ramp swings out from the island. With, I think it was, yes, it definitely is, Little Mquader the invader knocking Andabatus clean off his horse.

'The referee blows his whistle, and what's this? Yes, he has sent Andabatus to the sin bin, folks. He has definitely sent him to the sin bin, much to the cheers of the children in the crowd. Meanwhile, the mascots have regrouped, trapping the rest of the Gladiators in the pit. But wait a minute? What's this? Retarius has thrown his massive net over two of the mascots and the rest of the Gladiators are climbing up it and out of the pit. He pulls back on the net and the two mascots fall in head first, and down they go. All the other Gladiators and mascots are now slugging it out in the arena, except for the two mascots and Retarius down in the pit.

'Retarius does not seem to bothered; he is laughing his head off in fact. But wait a minute? The referee has blown his whistle for something. Let's go to my colleague, Marc Anthony, down trackside.'

'I can't really see too much from here, but it looks like the two mascots are being sent to the sin bin. The referee has taken something off them, and it looks like, yes, it is, its peacock feathers, Charlie. Yes, it's definitely peacock feathers, back to you, Charlie.

'Well, how about that for dirty tactics? No wonder Retarius was laughing his head off, that had to be painful. Now let's get back to the action. It looks like the mascots have it all to do now. Dimachaerius and Essedarius have pinned two mascots to the ground; they are facedown, and what's this? The two Gladiators have cut the wires to the mascot's electric fans in their suits. What a dirty trick? On a hot, steaming day like this one, those guys could drop from heat stroke.

'Yes, and I thought so, the referee has seen it and both Gladiators are off to the sin bin. We are getting down to the nitty gritty now as Laquarius unleashes his rope and lassos two mascots by their ankles. He is dragging them facedown toward the pit. The other two Gladiators are fending off a mascot in a defensive mode and Laquarius has all the time in the world to take care of his victims. But here comes the spare mascot around the side, and it's a midge bomb striking Laquarius bang on the back of the head. The referee has blown his whistle; he is sending the mascot to the sin bin.

'But the fighting continues. Laquarius is wriggling about the ground frantically scratching his armour, and I thought so, this first competition of the day is finished, sports fans, the referee has sent them all off. The children in the crowd are roaring their heads off. I don't really think anyone heard the whistle, but there you go, it's over now and the crowd at last can let out their breath. It's just another day in Gladiator land, folks, and we will be back after this short interval.'

Meanwhile, Strathclyde police have turned up with fifty officers to arrest Tyrannous.

'Excuse me, officers? My name is Mr Connolly and I am the lawyer representing the Heritage Trust.'

'We have come to arrest the big guy and his mates,' said the officer in charge.

'I am sorry,' said Mr Connolly, 'but we have it on good authority that no theft took place as my clients were only retrieving what was rightfully their property. Besides, would you like to disappoint all these children?'

'Fair enough,' said the officer. 'We will patrol the arena, but we will be talking to your client after the event.'

Back to the commentator, 'Well, it looks like we are expecting some heavy action in the next bout, folks, as Strathclyde's finest surround the arena. We are about to get back to the action, folks, as the next pair comes out. This is a tag team event featuring the mighty Gilber and John the giant, who is actually smaller than Gilber, from team Gladigator, versus Velitus and Secutor. They're standing face-to-face and the whistle blows, and we are back with the action. Velitus is probing away with that long spear of his at Gilber's shield, but Gilber stands strong, growling away and barely acknowledging the blows. Meanwhile, Secutor and John the giant are testing each other out as well with a few blows, but both are covering up well.'

The children in the crowd are starting to shout 'Tommy tomato nose' over and over.

Meanwhile, down in the arena, 'Who are they shouting at?' Secutor asks John the giant.

'Well, it's your name they are calling, Tommy,' said John.

'My name is not Tommy.'

'Maybe not,' said John, 'but you do have a big tomato nose.'

Secutor goes berserk.

Meanwhile back up in the commentary box, 'Well it's Secutor opening up, and he is smashing his way forward, raining blow after blow down on John the giant's shield, pushing him further and further back toward the island. Gilber has just grabbed hold of the end of Velitus' spear, pulling him toward him, and it's an elbow right to Velitus' face. He falls to the ground as he relinquishes the spear. However, John the giant is suffering badly; he is on his knees and Secutor is about to strike a devastating blow. But in comes the spear from Gilber, knocking Secutor onto the island. Two of the Gauls have leapt out and tied a rope to the Secutor's ankle. John the giant strikes a blow with his sword into the bushes and, wow, a tree flies up and Secutor is catapulted right out of the arena.

'Meanwhile, Velitus has managed to crawl to the side of the arena and tagged Retarius whilst Gilber's back was turned. He throws his net over Gilber and enters the ring with a sidekick as Gilber is sent crashing to the ground, as the bell sounds for the end of the first round. We have got one round to go in this two round tag team challenge, folks, and Gilber is raging at John the giant for not covering his back. However, the good news is that Secutor appears to be all right. The local fire brigade is erecting a ladder to get him back down from the Auchinlea sports base roof. Seconds out and we are into the next round and Secutor has been replaced by Laquarius. Both Gladiators now carry long pitchfork-like sceptres.

'Gilber and John the giant are circling the two Gladiators, who are fighting back to back with their two forks jabbing away at their opponents' shields. Gilber lunges in and out, as does John the giant, both sides testing and probing. Someone's got to make a move and the Gladiators are holding their forks above their heads, almost inviting Gilber and John to come in close. It looks as if their tactic has worked, as both Gladiators drive their forks down. But their opponents both sidestep, and the forks drive straight into the ground. Gilber and John pull back on the forks, and they rebound, striking the Gladiators clean on the face and they are out cold. What a move! If anyone knows what it is like to stand on a garden rake, then that was it.

'Gilber has thrown Retarius' net over both of them and he and John are dragging them toward the island. Out jumps General de Gaul himself to tie a rope on to the net. You guessed it, and there they go, suspended high up in the trees, and this bout is over – or is it?

'All the other Gladiators have jumped into the ring. Gilber has run into one of the Gladiator programme's inflatable toys for shelter. John the giant is taking a pounding, but we can see Gilber bouncing up and down, and out he comes with two giant boxing gloves on. It's the bouncy boxing, folks, he was not hiding, he was gloving up. The crowd is going mad and Gilber is knocking the Gladiators down, ten a penny. The mascots are now all in the ring. There is chaos in the arena. Now the police are jumping in. The bell is sounding, but no one can hear. Gilber is screaming at Veletus. I am still standing! I am still here as five police officers pull him away. Velitus gets the handcuff treatment and he is pulled away as well.

'That's the end of the second bout, folks, but I would have to give that to team Gladigator, and the crowd thinks so, too. We will be right back after another short break.'

Up in the crowd, a party atmosphere is in full swing as they await the next bout, and its one of their favourites. A loud cheer goes up calling for the Agitators and the two Ricky-canos. The main event is just ten minutes away now, between those two legends, Gladiator and Tyrannous.

Let's get straight on with the next event, and it is the triple mega challenge,' says the commentator. 'Two hundred and thirty-two feet of doom. The contestants will have to negotiate the tunnels, the rollers, the walls, then climb up the cargo nets and down the chutes, and if that's not enough, they have to contend with the American-style blockers. Somewhere hidden amongst that is the Velcro sections, where your clothes could easily stick fast. I can tell from the roar, or should I say booing, from the crowd that the contestants are on their way. It's Velitus and Myrmillo for the Gladiators, and they are here, as a huge noise bustles out around the park. Its Agi and Tator, who together form that awesome duo of bedlam, the Agitators, followed close behind by their partners in mischief, Dan the man and Blondie, who form that dynamic duo. the Ricky-canos.

'The referee is giving them their briefing as they approach the start. Well, would you believe it? The two Gladiators have pushed the kids and the Agitators to the back of the queue. No wonder the crowd is booing. The whistle blows and Dan the man and Blondie run under the Gladiators' legs and go to the front. The Agitators have grabbed their ankles, and both Gladiators fall forward, and the Agitators jump on top of them and they are off and running, as well.

'What a cleverly worked move that was! Dan the man and Blondie hit the tunnels first, closely followed by the Agitators, as two very angry Gladiators trail them in last position. They are out of the tunnels and the Ricky-canos hit the cargo net. The Agitators jump and bounce over the top of them and land on top of the chute. As they move into the lead, Velitus catches Blondie by the ankle halfway up the cargo net.

Dan the man drops down with a full body slam onto the head of Velitus, sending him crashing down on Myrmillo, as he somehow manages to hang onto the top of the cargo net. Blondie is on his way down the chute as the Agitators have just come through the rollers. The two Ricky-canos run and bounce clear over the rollers as the Gladiators smash clean into them.

'They climb over the rollers, and what is this? The Agitators were waiting for them, as they go into their famous spin and swipe the legs clean away from the Gladiators. It's now the Ricky-canos in the lead as they pass through the American-style blockers. The Agitators are in the blockers, closely followed by the two angry Gladiators. They're all in the blockers! The Agitators are out the other end. They are about to be caught, and, wow! The Ricky-canos had pulled the last two blockers back and released them, hitting the two Gladigator's full smack in the face and down they go, flat on their backs.

'They are all over the second chute and heading for the home straight. But they are now approaching the mega chute, and the Ricky-canos are about to climb the cargo net. The Agitators bounce and land above them. They are all approaching the top of the net, but the Gladiators have cut the anchor ropes. They pull on the net and the Ricky-canos and Agitators all fall to the bottom. The Gladiators are tying them into the net as the crowd boos. The Gladiators are now running on, unopposed, as they head for the sticky wall Velcro part of the course.

'But, wait a minute! What is this? It's Gladesgator and Lizzy doll making a beeline for the assault course. They are both screaming as they enter the arena. The crowds are reaching for the ear plugs that were supplied in their goodie bags. The Gladiators grab their ears and lose their footings. They fall onto the Velcro blockers and they are stuck fast. Gladesgator comes steaming through and lands on top of them. She is pounding away on the blockers as the Gladiators continue to fall down, only to pop back up again, sticking to the air-filled blockers.

'Meanwhile, Lizzy Doll has released the Ricky-canos and Agitators. They all bounce over the Velcro blockers and they're on the home straight. The Gladiators set themselves free and barge through the blockers and they catch the Agitators and Ricky-canos by the ankles at the top of the last cargo net. They only have to slide down the chute to win. Glades and Lizzy doll jump on both the Gladiators' backs, but still they won't let go of the ankles. But what's this? Here comes squadron leader Stephen, swooping down with the wing bandits. They are buzzing away and pecking at the Gladiators' heads.

'Now here comes Fraser the falcon, swooping on down the middle, and it's a midge bomb, right on top of the Gladiators' head. They release their grip. The Agitators and Ricky-canos slide down the chute together and its over! When have you ever known Fraser the falcon to get involved? He is normally only a scout. That was right out of the blue. The crowds are going mad, and it's another round to team Gladigator! Meanwhile, Glades and Lizzy doll are still jumping up and down on top of the Gladiators, who are to preoccupied with scratching their heads.'

'The crowd is cheering so loud, as Dan the man and Blondie take a bow; you can't even hear Glades and Lizzy doll. That's it, folks, we will be back in a few minutes for the big one, Gladigator versus Tyrannous, and they are first up in the chariot race. We will be right back after this break, and I don't think anyone would miss this one for the world.'

Meanwhile Alex approaches Lizzy doll down on the track.

'You know Gladesgator? But how?'

'Ah ha, Lecky boy,' she laughed. 'You should know Dan and Blondie tell me everything. I met her weeks ago.'

The triple Megga challenge in Auchinlea park on which the two Ricky canos and the Agitators defeated the gladiators

CHAPTER 13

The Final Conflict

'Welcome back to the big one, and the moment we have all been waiting for, folks, is only a few minutes away. It's the battle of the big two, the legend of Auchinlea himself, Gladigator, against the mighty Tyrannous. The atmosphere in the park is hotter than the blazing sun above. That's the setting for this most eagerly awaited event,' came the commentator.

Meanwhile down in the pits, 'This is it, Harry,' says Gladigator, 'once and for all.'

'What time is Tyrannous' pact with the devil due to expire?' asked Harry.

'I don't know,' said Gladigator, 'but Merlin told me there will be an eclipse of the moon and sun shortly before the event. But beware, it is a time when Tyrannous and his men will be at their most dangerous.'

'Now, listen carefully,' says Peacock Senior. 'Don't press the button on the left unless you want to see fireworks. I know about the two ejector buttons in the middle, but what about the button on the left?' asked Gladigator.

'Now is the time,' says Tyrannous, as he interrupts drawing his chariot alongside. 'Pass on the gift, and we can end this now, Gladigator.'

'He would not pass on the flu to you,' says Peacock Junior.

Tyrannous draws in a breath, leans over his chariot, and shouts, 'Boo!' followed by an evil laugh, and the two Peacocks scatter. 'I will deal with you lot once the victory is mine.' He scowled as he rode off to greet his pit crew.

Across at the other pit, Tyrannous starts to shows his nerves.

'I tell you all now, you had better fight like you never have before. If I lose, we all lose, and you will all burn in hell with me. You all know what to do.'

Back to the commentator, 'Well, they're all in the middle of the arena waiting for the big two. Gilber and John the giant stand waiting with the six mascots. Their menacing opponents, the Gladiators, are staring them down as if their lives depended on it. The crowd is on their feet, and here they come, riding side by side as they enter the arena, Tyrannous on the gleaming Real McKay, and Gladigator on the Rayton Rocket.'

'Now, remember what happened at the start of the race in the Circus Maximus? This guy will come at you from the gun,' said Harry.

'Who said anything about waiting for the gun,' roared Gladigator.

Back to the commentator, 'They're waiting for the gun, and wow, Gladigator catches Tyrannous by the back of his neck with his tail and pulls him clean off his chariot. There goes the starting gun, and the Rayton Rocket bullets away. Tyrannous re-enters his chariot and he is away trailing far behind. Four Gladiators jump in front of the Rayton Rocket to try and divert and slow it down, but out comes Gilber with a saber toss, and knocks them down like skittles. You can tell he has eaten his porridge this morning.

They're coming down the straight toward the island and Gladigator has a clear lead, with Tyrannous falling in behind. But what is this? Tyrannous is throwing razor sharp silver stars; one, two, three, four, they are all embedded into the back of the Gladigator's armour. Gladigator looks behind him and blocks another four stars with his shield.

Meanwhile, down on the track, 'Head for the island, Harry, I will meet you at the other end.'

The Gladigator presses the ejector button and flies onto the island.

Tyrannous is coming up to the island and the Gauls swing out the corves with Gladigator on the end of it. Tyrannous sees it just in time. He swerves, but not before Gladigator swings down his ball and chain, and rips the side clean off Tyrannous' chariot as it heads into the bend. The Gauls swing the corves the opposite way as the Rayton rocket is just coming out of the opposite bend. Gladigator runs down the corves and re-boards. He is off into the straight.

Back to the commentator, 'Tyrannous comes out of the bend, and, pow! He hits the corves head on. He is sent spinning over the top and miraculously re-lands, purely by chance, in his chariot, and he is out of it. He doesn't know where he is. What about that old ball and chain move? If there is one thing Gladigator knows about, it's the old ball and chain. He is an expert; he is certainly not married to Gladesgator for nothing, you know, folks.'

Meanwhile, down on the track, 'How was that for you, Harry?' shouts Gladigator.

'For a first lap, you're improving, I will give you that,' said Harry. 'But you are doing it again! Stop waving to the kids and keep your mind on the job.'

Just at that moment Retarius appears from nowhere and throws his net over Gladigator, pulling him straight off his chariot backwards. He drives his fork down, and Gladigator rolls away from him, straight into the path of the real McKay, carrying an unconscious Tyrannous. He rolls back toward Retarius, narrowly escaping the wheels of the chariot. Retarius prepares to drive his fork down for the second time.

Back to the commentator, 'And it's a sider from Gilber, knocking Retarius out cold. He picks Gladigator up and tells him to concentrate.

'The chariots are coming around for the second time, and so is Tyrannous, by the look of it, as he staggers back on to his feet. Gilber dips his knees and clasps his hands. Gladigator puts a foot in there and Gilber caber-tosses him. It's a backflip from Gladigator, straight back onto the chariot, as Harry the horse and the Rayton Rocket bullet by. Right behind them is Tyrannous' chariot as he holds out a shield and Gilber is sent spinning to the ground. There goes the hooter to signal the pit stop as both the chariots make their way in.'

Meanwhile, down in the pits, 'Okay guys, go to work,' Gladigator shouts as he jumps off to reload his weapons.

Scot the giraffe hoists up the chariot and the Peacocks go to work. Ram Ses shoves the hose into Harry's mouth. 'This guy is not concentrating,' says Harry, inbetween sucks on the hose.

'Why are you lifting the chariot up, you mug? There is nothing wrong with it,' says Peacock Senior.

'Who are you calling a mug?' asked Big Scot, as he drops the chariot, narrowly missing the two Peacocks.

Bible Billy throws a shoe, hitting Harry on the head.

'What do you think you are doing? Did I ask for a shoe?'said Harry.

'Who's mind is not on the job now?' asked Gladigator, as the crew falls apart. 'Get it together, you lot.'

Just then the Agitators jump into the pits.

'Okay, Pops, can we get money to buy a hooter?'

'Not now, guys,' said Gladigator. 'Can't you see I am busy? Why don't you ask the Ricky-canos' dad?'

'Some referee he is, Pops,' said Agi, 'in fact, some weightlifter as well; he has been lying out cold since the first lap.'

Gladigator shouts, 'Check?'

The crew shouts, Check!' and Harry the horse comes bulleting out of the pits in a record time of forty-two seconds.

Back to the commentator, 'Gladigator is out first, but what is this? There are four Gladiators firing silver stars; they are peppering Gladigator's chariot.'

Down in the arena, 'I don't know what the left button does, Harry, but here we go.'

Back with the commentator, 'Wow! And the Gladiator chariot opens up with blow pipes firing pitch balls of flame. The Gladiators' shields are ablaze. They drop their shields and swords and make a run for it. But all this activity has slowed Gladigator's chariot down, and out of the pits comes Tyrannous, closing in on Gladigator.

'He cracks his whip, wrapping it around Gladigator's wheel; it recoils and propels him forward, and he has landed in Gladigator's chariot. They are standing toe-to-toe as Steve the stallion heads off with the real McKay in the opposite direction.'

Meanwhile, down on the track, 'I can't hold on in this bend,' shouts Harry. 'Get rid of him!'

'I am trying,' says Gladigator.

Back to the commentator, 'They are trading blow for blow as they come up to the island, and Harry the horse goes one way and the chariot carries straight onto the island. Gladiator and Tyrannous fly through the air and land amongst the dense trees. The trees are beginning to shake and waver; the Gauls vacate the island like a plague of locusts.'

Suddenly, everything goes calm. The crowd is on the edge of their seats as a small rustle is seen in the bushes. Gladigator steps off the island to the cheers of the crowds. Suddenly, the Gladiators attack, but Gilber and John the giant are in hot pursuit. There is still no sign of Tyrannous as sporadic battles break out all over the arena. The Gladiators are fighting like their lives depend on it. The mascots have fallen one by one; down goes John the giant. Gilber and Gladigator are back to back.

All of a sudden, it happened – shadows start to appear.

'I don't understand it, says the commentator. 'There are no clouds, but I am gob smacked, it's an eclipse of the sun!'

However, down in the arena, Gladigator and Gilber are having a serious talk.

'Walk away, Gladigator,' says Gilber.

'I have waited 1900 years for this. Really, there is nothing you can do,' said Gladigator. 'These are forces you cannot understand; I am the son of Verceingertorix and I feel his power at this moment swelling my veins.'

The eclipse climaxes, pitching the whole park into darkness. After a few minutes, the first chink of the sun shines through, creating a faint twilight. Gladigator can see the faint outline of the Gladiators standing before him, with Tyrannous in the distance. Then, as the light begins to grow, Gladigator's sword glows in the dark. Laquerius throws his fork at great speed at Gladigator, who sees it at the very last moment, and moves his head slightly to the side as it narrowly whizzes by. Gladigator sends his shield spinning through the air, knocking Laquerius to the ground. He tries to stand up, but suddenly he turns to an ash-like statue. The tidal breeze of the moon sweeps in, and he turns to powder and evaporates.

Gladigator refocuses and walks on. He is surrounded by Dimachaerius, Andabatus, Retarius, and Essedarius. They all charge toward Gladigator with their swords drawn. Gladigator jumps in the air in a spiral motion, the sword on his tail cutting through their chest plates like a propeller blade. They all fall to their knees and turn to ash-like statues. Gladigator waves his mighty tail in a spiral motion a second time, and the tail wind turns them all to dust.

Gladigator continues to move forward. The twilight is starting to brighten, but the crowd still cannot see. Forward come Samnite, Secutor, Velitus, Myrmillo, and Thracian. They go into a classic defensive tortoise mode with three shields at the front and two at the back, holding their shields above their heads. There stands Gladigator, probing away, searching for an opening. The light is becoming brighter; he does not have much time left, therefore he charges.

The gap opens up to allow him into the trap. Gladigator has an advantage – he is left–handed. He also has a mighty tail. In he goes to the tortoise formation. He receives a blow, cutting through his shoulder, as the ball and chain is wielded upward and down from his mighty tail and two shields fall. The three remaining Gladiators thrust down with their swords, and Gladigator blocks two with his shield, just as the third sword crashes into the ground, narrowly missing his head. He springs to his feet and cuts his sword from the side across two of the Gladiators' waists and they fall to the ground. Velitus runs in fear. Gladigator picks up the giant spear that Velitus was famous for and throws it at lightning speed, pinning Velitus to the ground.

The tidal moon's breeze blows his ash figure to dust as Gladigator turns and swaggers his tail through the two other ash figures on either side of him, turning them to dust. He continues his walk forward and there is only one man left to face. The light is all clear now, and the crowd can at last begin to see. Tyrannous rushes toward Gladigator, who chinks to the left, but Tyrannous' sword catches him on the side as he rushes by. They both turn to face each other. Once again, Tyrannous rushes in, and Gladigator reverts to a childish trick he taught the Agitators. He spins around, hits the deck, and swipes the legs from Tyrannous as he rushes by. He falls facedown onto the dirt. He pushes out his arms and springs himself onto his feet as Gladigator jumps on his back. Tyrannous dips his knees and drives his mighty thighs upwards, sending Gladigator through the air and he comes crashing to the ground. Tyrannous turns at great speed and dives on top of Gladigator.

In a split second Gladigator pulls his shield in front of him to defend himself and Tyrannous lands on top of the spear head protruding from the centre of the shield. Silence descends upon the crowd as Tyrannous lies on top of Gladigator, mortally wounded. As his body slowly turns to ash, his last words are, 'We will meet again, Gladigator!'

'Never!' comes the reply, as Gladigator draws a mighty breath and blows into Tyrannous' eyes.

In an instant he turns to powder and crumbles. At the moment, the sun burst through in all its glory. The crowd doesn't know what to think. They did not see what happened to the Gladiators, but did they just see Tyrannous turn to dust? They knew the eclipse was real, but the Tyrannous thing just had to be an illusion. Slowly, but confusedly, the crowd began to clap. They started to chant Gladigator's name. After all, was this not what the day was about? Creating another Glasgow legend whose name would rank alongside St Mungo and St Stef. Would not, one day, the Gladigator name not grace the Glasgow coat of arms as the gator that never aged?

The world would never know what a debt it owed to the Glasgow Gladigator, or how he protected them from evil. But that's the thing about legends – you are only a legend hundreds of years after you are gone.

But today was still about the children of Scotland; we had a fun factory to open. The Gladigator crew stood back as the dignitaries made their way to the fun factory.

'I would now like to ask Baillie Catherine McMaster to open this fun factory for all of Scotland's children,' said Councillor Coleman, to the cheers of the crowd. 'A new start for a new generation, a generation where magical things would happen, a generation of dreamers in the city of dreams.'

Gladigator stood in the middle of Auchinlea Park listening to the excited screams of the children of Glasgow playing in the fun factory, playing on the wavy chute, the dastardly drop to the ball pit, the trampolines and the swings, and ordering up the Gladys burgers from the healthy eating café. Above all is the happy sound of families spending time together.

He had just come through the ultimate time of the long nineteen hundred years of his life. But to the world it did not really matter. It occurred to him that no one should really seek credit for making children happy, you should just be born to do it. Meanwhile, whilst Gladigator was reminiscing, the Strathclyde police were searching the park.

'I don't care what it takes, even if we have to stay here all night,' said the head of operations.

'But, sir, we have recovered all the artefact weapons. Surely that is good news?'

'But what about all the poor gang members they put in hospital, you clown? Now find them!'

In the background, amidst the Gladiator Programme's staff dismantling the theme toys, and the park rangers dismantling the barriers, the Gladigator crew came together.

'Will we see you again?' asked Gilber.

'Wherever you are, I will be there,' said Gladigator.

'Well, you are here,' said Harry the horse, 'so we will stay also.'

With those words, they all turned and entered the Provan Hall perimeter wall one by one.

However, one of their group was still searching for where the rest had gone to, As one local radio report highlighted the following day, 'Park rangers have been trying to capture a giraffe in Auchinlea Park believed to have been left behind after yesterday's activities. The rangers say they have tried shouting out names like George and Jerry, but the giraffe just kept shaking his head. A short time later, the giraffe was said to have disappeared.'

So what about the Gladiator programme? Well, they achieved what they set out to do. The fun factory, backed up, of course, with the legend of Gladigator, proved a big success, and no matter when our great city of Glasgow faced hard economic times, all the children's services were looked after by the Gladiator programme. People came from all over Scotland. At first, because their children wanted to come for the fun factory, but as their children grew, the day of the gathering and the final conflict switched from being a fantasy to a legend.

Up at the Provan Hall house, a very old Steve Allan switched from telling stories of the lizard people to stories of Gladigator, and it helped, of course, that the fun factory and the mascots were just next door. The Heritage centre boomed, as well – suddenly history was no longer boring to the children, there was a Gladigator hero amongst it. As for the fun factory, Gladigator became much like Santa Claus, some of our guys would walk the park in the mascot suit and wave up to the kids in the fun factory, and the parents would go along with it and pretend they could not see.

But what of Gladigator and the Agitators as the years rolled by? Alex and Lizzy doll kept in contact, but they could see that Gladigator and Gladesgator were getting bored. The challenge and the fear of Tyrannous had kept them alive for close on two millenniums, but now they had lost their purpose and they wanted to move on.

One day, some many years later, they were walking with the Gladigators in the park. No one paid attention to Lizzy doll and Alex; they thought it was just two old people with dementia talking to everyone but themselves. Then it happened, just when Alex was sharing a joke with Gladigator, a stabbing pain entered his chest and shot down his arm. He kind of knew he was a goner and he could not complain, he had lived his life and achieved many things. Suddenly, Gladigator grabbed his arm.

'Let me pass my gift on,' he said.

Alex gasped, 'I could not ask you to do that for me.'

'No, you don't understand. We have been waiting for this moment. You and Lizzy doll are why we did not leave. We wanted to pass the gift on.'

The Rickey-canos, who by this point in time were fully grown men, were standing in the background, as were the ageless Agitators.

'Won't you miss your children?' Lizzy doll asked.

'No, its okay, Pops,' Agi interrupted. He understood that a mere mortal lifetime was only a heartbeat away.

'I have to go with him,' said Lizzy doll to Gladesgator.

'It is okay. I understand. I have to go with Gladigator as well.'

There in the Auchinlea Park the Gladigators kissed the Agitators goodbye. Both Alex and Lizzy doll did the same with the Ricky-canos. Alex embraced Gladigator and Lizzy doll embraced Glades. Suddenly, two transporter lights from the northern skies shot down and surrounded them.

Both Alex and Lizzy doll were absorbed like a sponge into the Gladigators' bodies. Then, like a thunder bolt, the two transporter lights shot off and they were gone, taking two souls with them. Both Alex and Lizzy doll's bodies felt full of life, the way they had almost forgotten when they were young. Only they were not in their own bodies, they were in the Gladigators' bodies. At the same time they felt a great sadness to be losing their friends.

The moment was disrupted by the Agitators telling the Rickey-canos, 'Don't worry, we are staying until you are ready and we will do the same for you.'

A few years passed and both Lizzy doll and Alex were standing at the Auchinlea pond with the Agitators. They spot their grandchildren playing with the Rickey-canos. They are giggling because they can see them and they assume their parents can't.

'Look, Daddy, can't you see? Can't you see the Gladigators?'

'No, pet,' replied Dan the man.

But unknown to the children, Dan and Blondie were not talking to each other, but to the Agitators beside them.

'But what about Harry the horse and Steve the stallion? What about the Peacocks and Ram Ses? Whatever happened to Fraser the falcon and Stephen the squadron leader? Or the wing bandits, Ewan and Jimi? Where did the little General de Gaul and Admiral Hector ever go to? What about Shazza and Big Scot the giraffe? Or Fitsy Mac Ferret and Claire Voyant? Who could ever forget Mcquader the invader and Lorraine the liberator? Where on earth could you hide John the giant and Gilber?'

'Well, we know they swore a pact not to leave and they were last seen walking into the great wall of Provan Hall. Legend has it that they stay in the wall during the day, but weird noises supposedly come from the fun factory at night.'

It was said it really came to life when the children left. Legend has it that they all would party with the Gladigators and the Agitators during the night. The Peacocks are arguing how many balls are in the pit during a routine safety inspection, Shazza the squirrel is sliding down the wavy chute, crashing into Lorraine the liberator and Mcquader the invader, inbetween skiving from the toy shop. Big Scot keeps trying to explain to Fraser the falcon, Stephen the squadron leader, and the wing bandits Ewan and Jimi that he will turn nasty if they don't stop landing on his back. Admiral Hector and the general are exchanging tactics on the cargo nets, whilst all the time Clair Voyant can't predict a thing. John the giant is asking Gilber to measure him.

'Yes, John, you have definitely grown, but you are still a little snot,' says Gilber.

Harry the horse and Steve the stallion are next door in the buggy ride department discussing days of old, particularly about when Steve used to work for the council. But the entertainment is second to none.

There is Fitsy Mac Ferret singing away in the middle of a duet with none other than Frankie Vaughan, entertaining everyone as they go about their business.

You have got the sun, so life is sunny, to make it fun, you don't need money.

Frankie is all decked out in his top hat and tails as he takes the lead.

What more do you want.

Frankie kicks his legs head high and dips his shoulder. He turns to the audience tipping his hat. He gives a cheeky grin, winks his eye, and says, 'You ain't seen nothing yet!'

All of a sudden, the voice of Peacock Junior is heard coming from the floor, 'Give us Roman in the Gloman!'

'Shut it, Thomas,' comes the reply from Peacock Senior.

The End